I0647610

Grey Area

13 Ghost Stories

~because life & death is never black & white~

Edited by

Nancy S.M. Waldman & Julie A. Serroul & Sherry D. Ramsey

Third Person Press, Cape Breton, Nova Scotia

First Published in 2013
Compilation © Third Person Press 2013
Introduction © Ken Chisholm 2013
Cover © Nancy S.M. Waldman 2013
Copyright in the individual stories remains the property of the authors.
Interior Layout by Nancy S.M. Waldman

All rights reserved.

No part of this book may be reproduced, copied, scanned, stored in a retrieval system, recorded or transmitted in any form or by any means without prior written permission of Third Person Press, except by a reviewer, who may quote brief passages in a review.

The publisher does not have any control over and does not assume any responsibility for author/contributor or third party websites or their content.

This book contains works of fiction. Names, characters, places and incidents are the products of the authors' imaginations. Any resemblance to actual persons, living or dead, events, entities or settings is entirely coincidental.

Third Person Press
Email: thirdpersonpress@gmail.com
Web: thirdpersonpress.com
Cape Breton, Nova Scotia, Canada

Grey Area: 13 Ghost Stories
Print Version ISBN: 978-0-9811025-8-0
Electronic Version ISBN: 978-0-9811025-9-7

Dedicated to our loved ones gone beyond.

May they all be resting peacefully in a colourful place.

Also from Third Person Press

THE SPECULATIVE ELEMENTS SERIES

Undercurrents

Airborne

Unearthed

Coming in 2014: Flashpoint

OTHER TITLES

To Unimagined Shores,

Collected Stories by Sherry D. Ramsey

Stories

Introduction

Your User's Guide to Being Dead

Congratulations—you are dead!

What? You're not? That's what they all say. Yes, we've heard that excuse before: my kids need me, my wife will marry that schmuck from accounting if I'm not around, I have to save my cousin Englebert from that falling boulder, I haven't finished taking my bloody revenge on everyone who ever wronged me. Trust me, everyone has unfinished business in their life they need closure on. Last week, we had a 110-year-old woman demand to be returned because she had never tasted sushi.

Without unfinished business, there would be no ghosts bothering the living and the afterlife would be a lot deader.

You're from Cape Breton? Yes, there are more dead people wandering around Cape Breton than there are people there with steady employment (one of our little jokes). There's the story of the old fellow whose best friend came back to him after he passed, pestering him endlessly. "What do you want, John Angus?" the old fellow finally asked him. "I owe Hector the Butcher three dollars for a rump roast," the spectre replied. "Can you stand me for it?"

That is why a book of ghost stories with a Cape Breton connection like *Grey Area* is probably the best guide to being dead one could hope to have.

So, if you're reading this, it means you have bought, borrowed, or stolen a copy of it. If it's stolen please take the D express escalator immediately. That's "D" as in "Down" or "Damned" or "Dante". Attendants will guide you to your proper circle of confinement (right next to the one for illegally downloading copyrighted material).

Now, just because you are dead is no reason to lose your optimism. Like the characters in Nancy MacLean's tale, "Revenant," and Diane J. Sober's "This Is My Land," you might actually find being dead a romantic experience. As in "Mildred Mudd's Epiphany" by Charlotte Musial, being dead can help someone else appreciate the joys of living.

All right, there has been a lot in the media about, let's say, the more violent and sinister aspects of the metabolically challenged community. They're prone to acting out, give neighbourhoods a bad name, and according to one highly exaggerated movie, tend to make suburban houses implode upon themselves. "Letters To Mom" by Julie A. Serroul, about a violent ghost dad, and "Teetering on the Edge" by Voula Kappas-Dunn, about a ghost doling out some hard love, sort of support that idea, but go beyond the usual tabloid clichés.

But on the other side of the scales (and yes, we still use scales to decide things over here), "A Glimpse of Light" by Meggan Howatson offers a lovely farewell scene, while the deeply romantic "My Mews" by Nancy S.M. Waldman and the dreamy "Night Swimmer" by Leah Noble show that some things do survive death, often in unexpected ways.

"Out of the Deep" by D.C. Troicuk takes readers into the workings of a coal mine during a mining disaster, which is dire enough before adding the afterlife. "Not on This Earth" by Theresa Dugas offers that chill of apprehension everybody occasionally feels looking through an old family album when all of the faces, some more than others, seem uncomfortably familiar (especially Cape Breton photo albums).

Sherry D. Ramsey's "ePrayer," about a ghost literally caught in the machine who needs some computer assistance, seems like a bit of whimsy with its automated prayer machines, but trust me you do not want to meet our IT guys. You think the living ones are creepy.

And if you are looking for a story with teeth—the actual bite-y kind—then Hugh R. MacDonald's "Stillborn" has it. It would make a great short film (and perhaps it already has).

Finally, there is the tale that gives this collection its title, "Grey Area" by Katrina Nicolson, where a young man, who has made all of the wrong choices in life, is faced in death with new choices that are definitely more important and urgent.

Thirteen tales of ghostly significance.

You're dead already so you don't have to be worried about how scary they are. If you were still among the breathing, I'd say they are not to be read on rainy, windy nights. Not to be read when alone in a dark, creaking house miles into the woods. Not to be read when you suddenly remember a departed relative, friend, or lifelong enemy, who might have some unfinished business with you.

What's that? You are still alive? And you're happy with that? Oh.

In that case:

Boo!

Ken Chisholm
August 2013

KEN CHISHOLM lives in Sydney, Nova Scotia, and has written (by himself or in collaboration) over two dozen one act plays, hundreds of book, movie, and play reviews, and presently writes a weekly arts and culture column for the Cape Breton Post. He is also a long time member of the local theatre community as a writer, actor, and director. Two of his short stories have been published in anthologies published by Third Person Press, *Airborne* and *Unearthed*. In the afterlife, he plans to continue to haunt a favourite coffee shop.

Letters to Mom

Julie A. Serroul

Sometimes I write a letter to Mom in my head. *Hi, Mom, it's me, Michael. How are you? I'm fine. Right now I'm living with a ghost and a murderer....*

After that it just gets weird and hard to explain, so I usually stop the letter in my head. I can't send it anyway because I don't know where Mom is. I asked Dad once.

"Dad," I stared out the window of the car so I couldn't see any scary looks he might give me. "Could I...maybe, just send Mom a letter?"

My head hurt in two places after that, one where he'd slapped me and one where it had bounced off the car window. I didn't ask him anymore, even though I was pretty sure he knew where she was, or at least where she had been the night he stole me back. That's what he called it—he "stole" me back.

I try to remember. I remember the apartment, the building, the playground at the end of the street—even the walk to school. But those two blocks could be anywhere in the world because I don't remember anything else. I remember Mom teaching me our new address. It was the fourth time we'd

Julie A. Serroul

moved. I'd started to fill it in my journal at school too, on a sheet called "All about me." I just can't remember anything else. But I was only eight and it was a new address. That was three years ago.

My life so far is broken into a bunch of parts. There's the part with Mom, which was happy, except all the moving around. There's the part with Dad, which was scary all the time. And then there's the part when Dad got a new girlfriend named Sandi. That was okay—at first. And then, of course, there's the "now", where I live with a ghost and a murderer. I don't think much about the time with Mom because my stomach starts to squirm with about a hundred snakes. I told Sandi about that one time, when she was still Dad's "new" girlfriend.

Her mouth was pulled down as she looked at me with her eyes squinting a little. "Why a hundred?"

"I don't know. Feels like a hundred, at least."

She smirked. "I don't think a hundred would fit in your little belly...maybe a dozen, if they were really small." She wiggled all ten of her fingers and made a hilarious face.

We started laughing like crazy.

Dad yelled from the living room. "Keep it down!"

I covered my mouth with both hands to smother my giggles, but Sandi threw her head back and laughed louder.

Dad smacked the door to the kitchen open. "Do you two idiots mind? I'm trying to watch TV in here!"

I lowered my head and stopped laughing. My giggles were swallowed by the return of the hundred squirming snakes.

Sandi chuckled once. "Geez, someone's having a bad night." When she looked at me, her smile faded away.

She pulled her chair closer. "Let's look at that math question again." That's all she said, but I noticed her looking at the door to the living room a lot.

That happened after she'd moved in. She'd had to because her pipes burst at her apartment.

"Temporarily," she said.

Letters to Mom

I never told her that a few nights before I had seen Dad putting away his big wrench, or that the bottoms of his jeans had been soaked.

He was a lot different after she moved in, not so nice all the time. Sometimes he was really nice, but only sometimes. The other times there was yelling and hitting. Sandi changed too. She was less and less fun and then she started jumping at noises, or if she didn't hear me coming. Mom had been jumpy like that too.

One day after school I found her crying on the bathroom floor, rocking back and forth. Her makeup had streaked off in places. I could see a purple bruise in the stripes.

"Sandi, are you okay? Where's Dad?" I dropped my schoolbag and knelt down on the floor with her.

"Gone." She sobbed and turned to look at me. "What am I going to do?" Her eyes were wide and kept jumping from me to the walls, from me to the walls. Like she thought the room was going to squash us. "What am I going to do?"

I didn't know what to say.

"It's not just me anymore. It's not just me!" She jumped to her feet. "I have to get away from here, away from him."

I nodded, but my heart started thumping at the thought of being alone with Dad again.

She got really still and stared at me.

I looked back at her.

She put her hands on my shoulders. "I won't leave you here unless you want me to."

"No!" I threw my arms around her waist and started to cry. I'm embarrassed when I think about that, but I was only ten. I'm eleven now.

A few weeks later, Sandi picked me up from school with our suitcases in the back seat. She was shaky and said she didn't want to talk for a while. She kept driving even after it got dark. I didn't mention that I was hungry, but just when I was getting tired she seemed to remember that we didn't eat yet.

"Oh, geez, Mikey, I'm sorry. You're probably starving."

She ran into a gas station and came out with a couple of sandwiches and bottles of juice. "Sorry, only ham and

Julie A. Serroul

cheese left. I know you don't like the cheese, just pick it off, okay?"

She only had two bites of hers when she started crying.

I stopped chewing and became really scared that she wanted to go back. I grabbed her arm, "He'll be crazy mad if we go back!"

She threw her sandwich on the seat between us and started the car. "We're not going back."

In our new apartment, in our new town, Sandi cried a lot. Once I found out she was pregnant, I thought that maybe pregnant ladies just cry all the time, but then, when Dad showed up, I knew why she was crying so much.

He was crazy angry all right. He had a big cut across his head and his neck looked funny. He started screaming and yelling as soon as he came in, but Sandi just kept making our dinner.

I watched him screaming. I knew he was screaming because his eyes were bulging out and his mouth was open wide, but no noise was coming out. I was scared at first until I realized he couldn't hurt me. Then I felt better.

Then I felt bad, because probably I should have been sad that he was dead. But I wasn't. He stayed around for a long time, screaming and yelling, following Sandi around. Most kids would probably be scared of a ghost Dad, but my Dad was a lot scarier alive than he was dead. I didn't like looking at him because the snakes would start up a little in my belly. I think it was because I always felt bad that I didn't feel bad.

Sandi still cried all the time and her belly was getting really big. I worried that all her crying was making the baby feel sad, so I decided to tell her something I'd never told her before.

I brought her a tissue.

"Thanks, buddy." She blew her nose.

"Sandi," I rubbed my fingers over her bedspread, turning more toward her so that I couldn't see Dad screaming at the foot of the bed.

"Yeah, Mikey?"

⚉ Grey Area ⚉

Letters to Mom

Part of me wanted to tell her that I knew Dad was dead and why I knew, but I was scared she'd think I was crazy and leave me all alone. So I told her something that I thought might make her feel better about being a murderer.

"You know, Sandi...about my Mom leaving Dad and I..."

That's what Dad had told her. That Mom ditched us.

She put her hand on my hand. "Buddy, I understand now why your Mom ran away from your Dad. I do. And...and I bet she wishes every day that she'd taken you too." Sandi didn't look at me for the last part. Some grownups don't look at you when they tell lies.

"No. Mom didn't take off, Sandi."

She looked at me funny.

"I was only with Dad for about a year when you guys started dating."

Her eyes got really big.

"Mom ran away and took me with her when I was just a little baby. We hid and hid, because Mom said Dad would never stop looking. She said it was because of me. That he thought I belonged to him. She said I belonged to myself. But she was right about Dad, when he took me he said he was stealing me back...like I was a car or something."

Sandi didn't say anything, just squeezed my hand. Then she got quiet and put a hand on her big belly and looked down at the baby bump.

But the spooky thing was the way Dad acted. He wasn't jumping around or moving as much as usual, so I looked over at him. He had stopped screaming at Sandi and started staring at me.

Sandi didn't cry at night anymore and Dad didn't scream anymore, just followed me around creeping me out.

Sandi was at work one day after school and I was in the apartment not answering the door or the phone unless it rang once and hung up, which meant it was Sandi calling from work to check up on me.

Dad was floating around freaking me out when I said, "I'm not going to let you scare the baby when it comes, so don't even try. And I'm really glad you can't steal me or the baby

Julie A. Serroul

back from Sandi." I didn't look at him when I said it, but after a while I did.

He was crying. He kept crying and crying all that day.

Late that night, when Sandi was asleep, I woke up and Dad was at the bottom of my bed. He wasn't crying anymore. I sat up. He pointed at the wall and when I looked I could see our basement, like a movie was playing there.

I saw Sandi pulling our suitcases out from under a dirty old blanket and some boxes. She was tucking money inside the outside pocket of one of them when Dad came in the basement door carrying a bunch of stuff. He looked at Sandi and then at the suitcases. He dropped all the stuff out of his arms, his face crazy mad. She ran up the stairs and he ran after her. She was almost at the top when he grabbed her sneaker. She kicked out her foot and he pulled his face back. When he did, he slipped, pulling the little white sneaker off her foot and falling all the way to the bottom. Sandi didn't come back down at first, just stood there saying something, but there was no sound in my movie. She came down the stairs real slow and looked at Dad. He had a big cut on his head and his neck looked funny. She walked in a real big circle around him, still saying something. She picked up the suitcases and put them by the door. She walked over to him and picked up her sneaker. She put it on and looked at his face. His eyes were open. She said something, but he didn't say anything back. She picked up the suitcases and went out the basement door.

The movie was over and Dad was looking at me crying. I started crying too. I cried because I was happy Sandi wasn't a murderer. At least, not an on-purpose murderer. She was a by-accident murderer.

I looked at Dad. He was harder to see. He was disappearing. He made a word at me with his mouth really carefully. I knew what it was. It was "sorry". Then he disappeared. I cried again, but this time it was because I did feel a little bit bad that Dad was dead.

After Lindsay was born—that's the name Sandi and I picked together—we were really excited but really tired. Our apartment was just one big room made into sections. There

Letters to Mom

was a kitchen section, a living room section and a bedroom section. Sandi and I had side by side little beds and after Lindsay was born, we put the bassinet in between our beds. The only other actual room we had was a bathroom. Lindsay cried a lot in the nights and woke us up. Even after a few months when she was bigger and in a crib, she'd cry and wake us. Sandi said she wasn't hungry, just lonely. But then Mrs. O'Handley came and things got a lot better.

The day the paramedics came and took Mrs. O'Handley out of Apartment #202, Sandi covered my eyes with one hand. Her other arm was holding Lindsay. I was carrying the groceries in. But her hand couldn't cover both my eyes, so I saw that the sheet was over Mrs. O'Handley's face too.

So now Mrs. O'Handley comes in the night and makes faces at Lindsay and makes her laugh and talk in baby talk. Mrs. O'Handley can't answer her, but Lindsay doesn't seem to mind. After a while Lindsay falls back to sleep. Plus Mrs. O'Handley stays with me after school. It's annoying that she drifts in front of the TV and won't let me watch until my homework's done, but I like her company until Sandi and Lindsay come home from work and the daycare.

Sandi says she has almost enough saved that we can move to a bigger apartment, plus she said she's going to save some money so we can hire someone to help me find my Mom. I love Sandi a lot. But I'm still excited about finding my Mom. I know she's out there somewhere. If she were dead I'm pretty sure she would have come to see me. Plus, Mrs. O'Handley shook her head "No" when I asked if Mom was dead. She seemed pretty sure. I'm not sure why she's so sure, but she is.

So, I can finish my letter to Mom now and lots of others that I can save and give to her when I find her.

Hi, Mom, it's me, Michael. How are you? I'm fine. Right now I'm living with a ghost and a murderer, and my new baby sister. I'm very happy, but I miss you....

♋ Grey Area ♋

Julie A. Serroul

JULIE A. SERROUL lives on the mystical isle of Cape Breton where anything can happen (on her computer, anyway). She has always loved the tradition of ghostly tales told by campfire or candlelight and often finds her fiction a reflection of that. "Letters to Mom" was first published in *Cover of Darkness*. She is currently polishing up a short story submission for an upcoming anthology by Third Person Press called *Flashpoint*, editing a fantasy novel for her eager collection of first readers (numbering 3), and entering the world of blogging with her new blog: *Poking Holes in Reality* at julieaserroul.blogspot.ca.

Out of the Deep

D.C. Troicuk

Leidekker woke with a splitting headache. That was all he knew for a time, the intense pain. And the darkness. When he could think, his thoughts were of Margie and her migraines. How she'd laugh at him if she could see him now, laugh with more than a hint of retribution for all those times he had accused her of making excuses to lie in bed all day, leaving him to cook supper, do the dishes, put the kids to bed.

The bed he was on now was hard as stone. Where was he, anyhow? He tried to move, couldn't. Must be one of those dreams, like he had when he was a kid. The one where he knew he was still dreaming, but in the dream he was trying to wake up. Yeah, it was just like that. Half-awake, half-aware of his surroundings. Not knowing where he was despite the uncanny sense of familiarity. Was it summer at Donnie's cabin? His mother-in-law's house on the mainland?

He tried to open his eyes, couldn't. He must have gotten royally pissed last night, slept like a rock. Maybe if he rolled over. That's what he used to do to bring himself out of his dream paralysis. Not this time. His limbs were lead weights. He

D. C. Troicuk

tried to call out to Margie, then to whisper, then to force out just a little moan. But, just as in that childhood dream state, his throat was frozen.

He drifted in and out of consciousness, riding the pain for what might have been minutes or hours. When he could, he tried to focus, to make sense of it all. The last thing he remembered was the nightmare—the wrath of God descending from on high.

He woke for real now, coughing. A stabbing pain in his chest made him cry out. He opened his eyes a slit. They admitted no light. He tried to bring his hands up to rub away the sleep crust. One arm felt dead—he must have been lying on it. He drew the other up with difficulty, freeing it from under a heavy bedspread that fell away like loose rubble. When his fingers found his eyes, he felt the flutter of his open lids on his rough skin. And still there was only blackness.

With a shot of panic, he was in full consciousness. He was blind!

"You there, Johnny?"

The weak call came from Gavin somewhere nearby. There were other voices too, moaning, crying out.

"What happened?" Even as Leidekker said it, the truth of the situation came over him. They were all in the dark.

"Just a little bump," Gavin answered, almost cheerful.

A "little" bump. A "little" blow-out of coal from the weakened seam, allowing everything around it to collapse into the working level of the No. 4 mine.

"You hurt, Johnny?"

Leidekker drew a ragged breath, tasting dust. His throat burned with it. He probed his chest with his free hand, exerted his leg muscles, straining against the blanket of rock that held him down. "Broken rib, I'd say. My legs are pinned. I've got a head like the devil's hangover."

"Geez," Gavin said. "If I knew you were going to be such a cry baby I wouldn't've asked."

"How about yourself?" Margie used to say it hurt her to think. He understood now what she meant. A wave of emotion hit him. Margie. Dennis. Nicole.

🍁 Grey Area 🍁

Out of the Deep

"I'm alive," Gavin said. "More than that? I'll keep you posted."

Farther down the wall, moaning gave way to swearing.

"Who's there?" Leidekker called out. The panic of others somehow eased his own.

A roll call came back to him. Fred. Tony. Jackie. Ray. Scooter. Bull. Others answering for themselves and for those who couldn't speak up.

"Archie's here too," somebody said. "Hurt bad."

Archie. A month shy of retirement.

Like Leidekker and Gavin, those who could were getting their bearings, worming themselves out slowly from under the debris, monitoring their movements, checking for broken bones, doing the same for those who couldn't do it for themselves. Somebody found a cap with a working lamp. The single weak light brought a cry of triumph.

Leidekker pulled himself up to lean against the wall and did what would be expected of him: he took charge. "Somebody has to go up above, to where it buckled," he said. "See what the story is."

"I'll go."

There was no mistaking that voice, high-pitched with fear. Scooter. Still a boy, really. He'd dropped out of school this year, proud as punch to get on at the mine, drawn by the pay. "Beats pumping gas," he'd said. Sad that he couldn't see himself doing more than that in life. Leidekker winced at the thought. At Scooter's age he'd had far bigger dreams—but where did they get him? They were in the same boat now. Scooter, a victim of a lax economy; himself, thanks to the family that came too soon. *Well.* He had no regrets on that score.

"Take the light," Leidekker told him.

There was a general grumbling. *Just make it quick.*

He watched Scooter's progress. In the aura of the lamp, the boy got smaller and smaller. And when he couldn't see it anymore, his eyes followed the memory of light, and held onto it, like hope.

🍂 Grey Area 🍂

D. C. Troicuk

If anyone trapped underground could be called lucky, they were. The bump had occurred some fifty yards up the slope from their position, by their estimation. The force of it had thrown rock into the working level. But they had been on the move, gathering for their lunch break, with full cans and thermoses. If not for this timing, they all would have been buried.

In the first hours, the instinct was to effect their own escape. Those who were able crawled like moles up the embankment of fallen stone to where the tapering gap ended, not in an opening as they hoped, but in a solid barrier. They kicked and punched trying to find a weak spot; they clawed and scrabbled until their hands were raw, called out until they were hoarse. They pounded stone on stone, and put their ears to the rock bed straining to hear a distant answering chink from the other side. But each attempt, starting in hope, brought only futility and desperation.

Those less mobile stretched out from where they lay or crawled about to explore their immediate surroundings. They collected scattered lunch containers and hard hats—a few with lamps intact—and splintered timbers and twisted pieces of metal that could be used as tools for digging or sounding out a message: *We're here!*

While Ray led the survivors in prayer, Leidekker thought ahead to more earthly matters. Fourteen men were accounted for, including him and two casualties. Even after turning a lamp on them, he could only guess who they might be.

"Ray," Leidekker said, "do you suppose you can say a few words over them?"

"I didn't think you were a religious man."

He wasn't. But he was a practical man. Decomposition would be accelerated by the heat down here, two miles underground.

Out of the Deep

   The sombre task of burial brought a pause to the frantic digging for freedom. Afterward, they sat altogether for the first time assessing their situation, dealing with the acceptance of it. They spoke of home and family, shared memories, dreams, regrets. Their spirits rose with renewed hope, and fell again into despair. When one broke down, another buoyed him up. They laughed. They prayed. They sang. And so it went, the interminable passage of day into night, two days, three days...

🐦

Leidekker set up a routine of sorts, rotating the men digging through the rock fall, doling out their lunch can rations, calling for rest periods. Returning from his own shift, he stepped over outstretched legs and suppressed a moan as he lowered himself cautiously to the ground. He turned off his lamp to conserve the battery. In the darkness, a sense of restlessness grew all around him and talk resumed on the subject he must have interrupted.

   He felt a nudge from the man sitting next to him. "Hey, Johnny. You see anything up there today?" It was Scooter, tentative, scared.

   "Like what?"

   Scooter shifted uncomfortably. "Fred seen a ghost or something."

   "I never saw nothing," Fred barked.

   "Heard, then. It told him we need to go into the deep."

   A chorus of derision arose. *For the love of God, Scooter.*

   "Ssh! What's that?" Scooter squealed with fright. "Listen."

   "Go down." The voice, weak and raspy, the words barely understandable, came from outside their circle. "You got to go down."

   Fred crawled toward the voice. "Settle down, kid. That ain't no ghost. That's Archie. How're you doing, Arch?"

   It was the first time the older man had uttered a sound. They could not move him but had made him comfortable where

D. C. Troicuk

they had found him, propping him up on a pillow of stones so that he could breathe more easily, though at times it didn't seem he was breathing at all. The rest of them had made camp, such as it was, farther down the wall—the working coal face—where the booms and timbers of the ceiling structure were intact. Now they gravitated toward him to hear what he was saying.

Fred leaned in close and repeated for the others. "We need to go down, he says. To the old Number Two mine. We can get out by the air shaft."

"The old Number Two?" Scooter said. "That was sealed. Wasn't it?"

A chorus answered in the affirmative.

But Archie, the only one of them who had ever worked in that section, disagreed. "Not sealed," he said, his voice rasping like his throat was filled with gravel, his lungs wheezing like he breathed through a wet sponge.

"You know what I heard?" Bull said. "The company got hold of one of them doors off a WWII submarine. Set her in where the air trap was."

Anger, irrational and unpredictable, bubbled up.

You're daft, b'y.

Swearing a blue streak, Bull defended himself. "I heard it myself. Up in the office. The General Manager was right there—"

"Settle down," Leidekker told them. He was fed up with the bouts of temper, though he was barely controlling his own. But it was up to him to set an example.

Archie spoke in short spurts, gaining strength, no longer needing Fred to pass on his message. "I'm telling yez. There's a hatch. A back door. A way out."

Leidekker scratched his head. Hope. They surely needed it. But it could be a dangerous thing too. "I don't know, Archie. We got no way of knowing what's on the other side."

"I'll tell you one thing," Archie said. "There's water. Seepage from an aquifer. Good water it is, too. I drank it myself."

Out of the Deep

Talking all at once, each man sounded a different argument. If Archie drank the water, it was years ago. If there was gas built up on the other side they could be admitting methane—tasteless, odourless, and deadly—to an environment that, so far, was relatively safe. And what if the old mine was flooded? What if by opening that man-door, if there even was such an opening, they faced death by drowning?

"No matter what's on the other side," Gavin said, "we're in a final countdown to eternity here, boys. We need to make a decision. Who's going, who's staying?"

It was clear they couldn't all go. Aiden could not be moved. Lonnie, his buddy, would not leave his side. Tony and Fred didn't think they could make it that far. Henry's faith in the draegermen could not be swayed. Again and again he reminded them, "I'm not bragging, but I was on the winning team in international competitions for seven years running. These guys are the best in the world. If anyone can get to us, they will."

Five of them got to their feet. When—not if—they got out, they would send a team back in the same way for the others. And still they hesitated, weighing the pros and cons. Leidekker knew what they were thinking. He was thinking it too. Gas. Flooding. Sour water. But was any of it worse than sitting there waiting to die?

Archie spat. "You fellas can curl up like little girls and wait for the big strong draegermen to pull yez out. But I'm not gonna lie here and let yez all die. So, follow me or don't, but I'm going down." A lamp came to life, a lamp on a cap suddenly planted on Archie's head. Rather than focussing ahead of him, the glow poured downwards, encompassing him in an aura of light.

Leidekker swore under his breath. The old skunk had kept another lamp all to himself. For what? He'd never even turned it on before now.

It was a miracle that Archie could move at all, but he braced one hand on the wall, took a minute to balance himself, then moved into the dark tunnel with a straight back and a steady gait.

☘ Grey Area ☘

D. C. Troicuk

The men organized quickly. The five men made a chain, each putting his hand on the shoulder of the man in front of him. Leidekker, in the lead, switched off his lamp to conserve the battery and relied on Archie to guide them. But as injuries slowed their pace, Archie forged ahead tirelessly, increasing the distance between them, and suddenly, the mine was pitch black once again. Leidekker stopped, feeling for the switch on his own lamp. The men behind him fell against each other like dominoes. He called out to Archie, but got no reply.

His lamp was dimming, but adequate. The beam fell on something set into the wall up ahead. "Holy Christ," he said. "What's that?"

The men gathered around it.

"That," said Gavin, who had served in the navy, "is a pressurized door lock off a WWII submarine."

"I told yez," Bull chortled. "Didn't I tell yez?"

"Archie!" Leidekker called out again. "Where the Jesus did he get to?"

"Taking a leak, I guess," Scooter said.

Bull was already pushing them aside. "Stand clear."

He grabbed hold of the wheel of the door lock and grunted with the effort of trying to dislodge the corrosion of two decades. Puffing like a steam engine building power, he put his whole body into it. They heard, more than saw, the opening crack, the hiss of an airtight chamber being unlocked.

Leidekker lit the passage as one after another the men stepped across the threshold into the old Number Two mine. Water trickled down the wall into a little pool and ran from there down the slope into the deep. Scooter flung himself down. Ignoring the excited warnings he scooped his hands, drank, and sighed with a deep satisfaction.

"Where did that Archie get to?" Leidekker said again.

There. A light up ahead.

"How the hell did he get up there?" Jackie said.

"Come on then," Leidekker told them. "We'd better keep up."

Out of the Deep

Fresh air. Leidekker breathed deeply. The night was black as pitch, starless; the air perfectly still. He tried to locate himself. And then he remembered. The air shaft. There should be a pond nearby, and the ocean below a thirty-foot cliff. But there was not a whisper from the sea. No crickets, no mosquitoes. As a teenager he had skated on that pond, shared hot chocolate and a sweet kiss with a girl who lived in the last house on the street. But where was the street? In the trauma of being reborn from the earth, he had lost his sense of direction—not north to south or east to west, but his grounding in space and time. A thought caught him off guard. *Had they emerged at all?*

But he breathed the sweet pure air, and felt the rough terrain and grasses and wildflowers that tangled around his feet, pulling him down. He collapsed willingly into the fragrant August field and lay on his back, laughing. He was alive. More than alive—he was out of that godforsaken hole. An urgency to see, feel, taste home and loved ones was replaced by an overpowering exhaustion that overtook him. He gave in to it and slept.

He woke to birdsong, his head pounding. Sitting up, he could discern the forms of black phantoms rising one by one out of a thick morning fog. His buddies. In the near distance streetlights glowed. Peaked roofs of houses nudged the pre-dawn sky.

Five men located each other, but not their guide. The consensus was that Archie, who lived nearby, must have gone directly home. They set off down the middle of Quarry Road to the colliery where, no more than a mile away, their wives and families would surely be waiting.

Their arrival at the pithead coincided with another commotion. There was a buzz of excitement in the crowd. All eyes were on the mine entrance. After days of waiting, the draegermen were bringing up the first of the survivors. Shouts and cheers went up as one by one the rescued were recognized and swept into waiting arms.

Grey Area

D. C. Troicuk

Coming from behind, Leidekker and the others fanned out into the crowd unnoticed at first. He caught sight of Margie's flaming red hair and called out. She did not hear. The din of voices, the purr of vehicles on stand-by, the hum of emergency generators combined with the familiar rattle of the cage being hoisted made his head throb.

Jubilation gave way to a hush. A wall of men closed in as if to conceal the stretchers being borne away. Leidekker pushed his way into the circle of EMTs and company men standing around an open body bag. One of the draegermen identified the man: "That's Archie Cameron."

Leidekker reached out to stop him from pulling the zipper closed.

He heard another identification as if from a great distance. "Johnny Leidekker! Where did you come from?"

He cringed under the stares and the congratulatory slaps on his back. Ignoring their questions he remained intent on the face masked in coal dust. He saw what they saw—the signature black T-shirt under red plaid flannel, the wild, furry eyebrows. And still he denied the truth.

"It isn't him," he said, wracking his brain, running the shift roster in his head. "It can't be. It was Archie that led us out. Up through the—"

"Not this fella," the draegerman interrupted. "He come up like this."

Leidekker's head swam. "We came out through the old Number Two and up the old air shaft. If it wasn't for Archie—"

A rush of people surrounded him, and he succumbed to the chaos, let it sweep him along through a hasty briefing cut short by a doctor who shone a light in his eyes and asked him stupid questions. *What day was it? Who was the Prime Minister?* Then an ambulance ride to the hospital and one test after another. And every time he opened his mouth to tell what happened, the skepticism, the pats on the back, the patronizing words of encouragement. *Hang in there, b'y. You'll be okay.*

🍂 Grey Area 🍂

Out of the Deep

Released into Margie's care, he was at last home in his own bed. Instead of the sanctuary he craved, he was frustrated by her stubborn refusal to hear him out and by her non-medical diagnosis that he had rattled something loose in his skull. Even worse was the endless swirl of questions inside his own head as he tried to mesh together the miracle he knew as truth with the logic of what others were telling him must have happened. From their room at the top of the stairs he heard his wife turning visitors away, taking calls on the phone in the hall, telling everyone the same thing: "Maybe in a few days, when he's back to himself." *When he comes to his senses*, was what she meant.

Against doctor's orders, he pulled himself together for Archie's funeral.

Archie's widow clung to him. "You were with him, were you, Johnny? At the end?"

"No, Grace," Leidekker said. "I didn't see him after we got out—"

"No, but underground. In his last moments?"

Leidekker looked deep into her eyes, seeking an understanding of his own. "If it wasn't for Archie, we'd have never got out. He's a hero in my book."

She took both of his hands in hers. "Thank you for that, Johnny."

Margie nudged her husband to move on. Behind them one of Archie's sons grumbled, "Hero? What's he talking about?"

Grace soothed her forty-year-old son like a child. "He's being kind, dear."

"He's a nut job is what he is."

Bristling with anger, Leidekker gave Margie a signal: *I'll wait for you outside.*

He passed Bull in the hall, on his way in. They nodded a mutual greeting. In the parking lot Gavin was having a smoke with Scooter and Jackie and Ray.

D. C. Troicuk

"What's going on?" he said, accepting a cigarette. He took a long drag, watching clouds scudding across a blue sky. "Have you boys told anybody?"

"Tried to."

"Nobody wants to hear it."

"Word has it we're all nuts," Jackie said.

"Speak for yourself," Leidekker said.

"Yeah, well, if you can make sense of it, let's hear it."

Gavin threw his butt to the ground. "Now, you know and I know—we all know, Johnny, what happened. But the boys and me have been talking. Maybe it wasn't exactly the way we thought. Now, wait. Just hear me out." He followed Leidekker's angry retreat toward his own car. "We were all injured, disoriented."

Leidekker stiffened, looked from one to the other. "What are you saying?"

Scooter hung back, studying a clump of grass growing through a crack in the asphalt.

"I'm saying—" Gavin shook his head.

"What he's saying," Jackie interrupted, "is you got to snap out of it and keep your mouth shut. There's no way we come up the air shaft. Not with Archie. Not with nobody."

"Look. I get it," Leidekker said. "I don't like the way people are looking at me either. Like I'm looney-toons. But just between us five, we *know*."

"Here's what I know. We couldn't get through to the air shaft. So we turned around and by the time we got back to the fall, the draegermen were after breaking through and getting the other fellas out. But we were down below, looking for the shaft. But we never found a way out, right? We came back and followed them out on our own, a few minutes behind. And then there was so much commotion on the surface, that must be why nobody saw us right away."

Gavin placed a firm hand on his shoulder. "That's our official story. We're all agreed."

"Bull, too," Scooter said.

"If you know what's good for you, Johnny," Jackie added, "you'll stick to it too."

  ☘ Grey Area ☘

Out of the Deep

Leidekker squeezed his hands against both sides of his head. Applying pressure eased the headaches, momentarily. "You know damn well that's not how it was."

Gavin opened the passenger door of his car. "Take a ride with us. There's something you need to see."

Standing in the open field Leidekker turned his collar up to ward off the chill. Was it all only a dream then? Some kind of hallucination? He looked for inconsistencies in the details of the landscape, the harbour, the town in the distance across the bay. Everything was just as it should be. He spoke to each of his buddies in turn, and each responded true to his own unique character. Humourous, timid, gruff.

Seagulls shrieked overhead. Below the cliff the ocean roared. He watched the fog creep in, watched as it thickened and blurred the chipped and faded graffiti painted on the solid concrete cap that sealed the air shaft of the Number Two mine.

D.C. TROICUK brings to her work a varied life experience that has taken her from Atlantic to Pacific and back again. Her work has appeared in literary magazines and anthologies, including other speculative fiction collections from Third Person Press. Her first collection of short stories, *Loose Pearls*, was published in 2010 by Cape Breton University Press. www.dctroicuk.ca

Revenant

Nancy MacLean

She blinks against stinging rain and tries to gather her scattering thoughts. The beam of a headlamp shines and she sees a crumpled car against the prostrate trunk of a tree. She grapples at her fleeting memory until recognition of the vehicle anchors her. It is the rental car she has driven from Halifax to this easternmost corner of Nova Scotia. Wind, rain, and nightfall had obscured the fallen tree until too late.

The piercing chill of the October wind steals through the trees to bite at her, and she forces herself to clamber over the tree to the road beyond. Relying on the feel of gravel beneath her feet to guide her, she ignores both the penetrating rain and the gnawing fatigue, determined neither will keep her from finding the soldier who has haunted her dreams for more than a decade.

She started dreaming about this man as a teenager, yet he always looked the same, standing at attention, his dark hair gleaming. She had considered him to be merely a figment of her imagination until yesterday when she spotted him in a photo in the *Toronto Star*. The paper claimed the man was Robert Collier. In the photo, his uniform was that of a

Nancy MacLean

policeman, not a soldier, but his dark, handsome features were too familiar for her to be mistaken. The accompanying article hailed the officer as a hero; he risked his life to save a youngster who had been swept into the ocean at Peggy's Cove. After pushing the youth to safety, the policeman was knocked onto the rocks by a wave and broke his arm in two places. If not for the rope thrown to him by the owner of the local gift shop, he would have been swept out to sea.

After reading the article she knew she had to find him. The first available flight brought her to Halifax this morning. She headed directly to the Halifax Regional Police headquarters where she learned Robert had gone to Cape Breton to recuperate at his family home. Twice she had to stop to ask directions and by the time she pulled into this narrow driveway, nightfall had stolen any light left by the storm.

She spots a tiny glow in the distance and anticipation propels her leaden limbs. As she draws closer, she sees that the illumination originates from an oil lamp perched in a lower floor window of an otherwise dark house. Feeling heavier and more tired with each passing second, she manages to climb the wooden steps. With numbed knuckles, she knocks, though the sound is swallowed by nature's tantrum.

The door opens. A tall man stands immobile, his features cast in shadow. When he pulls her inside, what energy she has left drains out of her. The warm strength of his arms is all that keeps her from crumpling to the floor.

Too soon he releases her.

She looks up, feeling a wash of disappointment. This is not Robert Collier, but someone much older, in his fifties perhaps, and wearing not a uniform, but a business suit. His strong resemblance to the man in her dreams makes her realize that this must be Robert's father.

His brows knit in puzzlement. "Where did you come from?"

"I— My car," her teeth chatter around her words, "hit a downed tree."

"Good Lord, are you hurt?"

🐚 Grey Area 🐚

Revenant

"N-no." At least she doesn't think she is. Just cold. So terribly cold. She tries to hug away the next shiver.

"You're drenched through. Let me get you some dry clothes."

He takes the lamp from the window and disappears up the stairwell, leaving her in a dark that feeds the cold eating at her soul. The ensuing silence indicates Robert's father is the only person here. Her disappointment threatens to deepen into despair.

He returns, holding out a bundle. "All I could find was this sweat suit of my son's." He lights a smaller lamp and hands it to her. "You can change in the bathroom just behind you."

The dated wallpaper that covers even the sloped ceiling of the small room tosses her into the past. She glances at her image in the mirror and it startles her. In what should be the flattering warm light of the lamp, she looks pale, distant.

It takes more than a little effort to peel off the windbreaker, shirt, and jeans that, in their sodden condition, cling to her like a second skin. Robert must be built like his father, she decides, as she has to roll up both the sleeves and pant legs and double over the waist. Instantly, she feels warmer and strangely safe.

When she leaves the bathroom, she finds Robert's father standing at the stove with his back to her. Broad shoulders strain against his suit jacket as he tries to shove a chunk of wood through the narrow hole in the top of the stove.

After setting a kettle to boil, he turns around and points to a chair. "I found some tea in the cupboard, but there's little else, I'm afraid. Rob only uses this place once in a while for hunting and fishing."

Rob. Her soldier. She sits down, trying to quell the impatience riding within her.

He leans on the back of the other chair and studies her with dark eyes that remind her of the man in her dreams. "So tell me, young lady, what are you doing way out here in the middle of a storm?"

&a; Grey Area &a;

Nancy MacLean

She swallows, then says, "I'm looking for your son."

His thick brows shoot upward. "You know Rob?"

She searches for words that she hopes will not cast doubt upon her sanity. "The *Toronto Star* ran a story about Rob rescuing a young boy at Peggy's Cove." She hesitates, as it is here that she must opt for fiction over fact. "I want to interview him."

"Interview him?"

"Yes, I'm a journalist." This comes out easily enough, as it is true. Her impatience makes her brave enough to ask, "And where is your son? His sergeant said he came here."

"Rob's on the other side of the island, fishing with a friend."

"With a broken arm? In this weather?"

A light comes into his eyes and the makings of a grin tug against his otherwise solemn features. "Oh, I doubt he's out in this. Besides," he bends one elbow repeatedly, "you only need one arm to do what they're probably doing."

She points to his suit. "And what about you? You aren't dressed for either fishing or hunting."

He sighs and she wonders what she has said that makes him look so sad. "I—I haven't been here in years. This afternoon I felt like going for a drive and, well, I ended up here." In an obvious attempt to change the topic, he says, "The lights went out just after I got here. I'll bet you dollars to donuts that tree you ran into took down the power line. Do you think I'll be able to get my car around it?"

She recalls the huge tree lying across the driveway and knows nothing can get past that. She shakes her head.

"Cell phones don't work out here. I guess we'd better wait until daylight before we try hiking into the village. From there, we can call a tow truck and let Rob know a pretty young lady is looking for him."

His tone has softened and there is warmth in his eyes. She feels herself blushing and glances away. When she looks back, he is still studying her.

"By the way, who should I say is looking for him?"

❧ Grey Area ❧

Revenant

She laughs when she realizes she hasn't introduced herself and then becomes alarmed when her name doesn't come to her right away.

His eyes narrow. "Are you all right?"

She laughs again, but knows it sounds forced.

"Yes, just a little stupid. Uh…Cassie…Cassie Pearson." *Journalist. Columnist for the* National Post. *Seeker of hunk from dreams.* She is thankful the whistling kettle diverts his penetrating gaze.

He sets a mug in front of her.

"The teapot is AWOL," he says, handing her a spoon, "so I just put the bag in the cup. Not a proper cup of tea, me mum would say. And I've no milk or sugar to offer you."

She smiles at the Scottish inflection that has snuck into his voice. "This is great. Thanks." Though her sip is small, the brew is quite hot and the warmth reaches her soul.

"So what do you do?" she asks.

He doesn't answer until he prepares his own cup of tea and sits down opposite her. "I'm a doctor. I spend most of my time doing the nursing home circuit in the Sydney area." His gaze locks onto hers once more. "So, Miss Journalist. You came all the way from Toronto just to interview my son?"

"I was in the Halifax area anyway," she lies.

"You drove all the way out here? In the dark, in this weather?"

"It was daylight and not even raining when I left." She shrugs. "I forgot how short the days are now."

"Do you have someone who is worrying about you?"

"No." She hopes this answer will suffice, but the arch in his eyebrows asks for more. "I only have my aunt and, well, we're not really close." Her adoptive parents had died when she was sixteen, forcing her to move in with her eccentric aunt. Cassie had never felt welcome in her aunt's home and had been happy to escape to university. She blinks into the present to find the dark eyes still studying her patiently.

When she adds nothing further, he asks, "What about co-workers, friends, or a significant other?"

❧ *Grey Area* ❧

"My work knows where I am and there is no one else."
After a few failed relationships, she has remained single. As
she entered her twenties, the dreams recurred with greater
frequency, each one leaving her with a longing as raw as an
open wound.

To divert the conversation, she says, "You haven't told
me your name."

He smiles and warmth slides across the table to her.
"Bill Collier." He spreads his arms. "Welcome to our
homestead. I grew up here, and for a few years my wife and I
used it as a vacation home. It belongs to Rob now."

Cassie feels much more comfortable in the role of
interviewer. "And your wife, she didn't want to come here with
you?"

His features stiffen, but not before the return of the
sadness she had detected earlier. "No. She passed away many
years ago."

He still loves her, she realizes, and she aches for
someone to feel that way about her.

He stands up. "Well, Cassie, perhaps we should retire
so we can get an early start in the morning." He hands her the
larger of the two lamps. "You can turn down the wick, but keep
it lit in case you need to get up in the night, as the only
bathroom is the one down here."

She reluctantly follows him up the stairs. At the top, he
points to a dark doorway at the end of the hall. "There are
extra sheets and quilts in the bottom drawer of the dresser."

She pads down the hallway. When she reaches the
room, she turns back to see him still watching her. He holds
his lamp at waist level, casting his features in shadow, much
like when he first opened the door. He looks so much like the
man in her dreams it is all she can do not to run to him. Then
he turns and disappears into the other bedroom.

She hastily makes the bed and crawls into it fully
clothed. The wind relentlessly throws rain at the glass as if
angry she has found refuge. Then she hears something else.
The gentle throb of surf. It sounds familiar, even soothing.

🍃 Grey Area 🍃

Revenant

Strange, she thinks, as she has never learned to swim and has always been afraid of water deeper than her knees. Her fatigue returns with a vengeance, so she snuggles beneath the sheets and lets herself be drawn into the comforting flame of the lamp.

☙

She leans back against the warm body lying against her and smiles. She is with her soldier once again. Heat radiates from his hand resting on her bare hip. He gently pulls her tighter against him and she can feel him become aroused. It all seems so real. She opens her eyes and is startled to discover the hand upon her hip *is* real, and the man lying next to her *is* aroused. *Rob?* She rolls away and up onto her knees.

It is not Rob, but his father, and her movements have awakened him. His eyes open wide when he sees her, then his arms flail as he tumbles backward off the bed. He scrambles to his feet and turns up the lamp.

Trying to suppress what she felt only seconds before, she blurts out, "What are you doing in here?"

Shock freezes his features until, after a quick glance about, his eyebrows knit in a frown. "Wait a minute, this is my room!" His deep voice is so loud she expects it to rattle the windows. "What are YOU doing in HERE?"

She realizes then that this is not the room she went to sleep in. She backs off the bed and stands up, discovering that somewhere in her travels she has left behind the sweatpants. Fortunately, the top is long enough to cover the most important parts.

"I—I'm so sorry. I must have been sleepwalking."

He points toward the open door. "Well, young lady, I suggest you sleepwalk back to your room and stay there." His harsh words hold both embarrassment and anger.

She hurries out. Behind her, the door closes with a definitive click.

☙ Grey Area ☙

Nancy MacLean

The pants lay piled on the floor beside her bed. Shivering, she pulls them on, longing to be warm like she had been just moments before. His hand felt so right.

She doesn't dare fall asleep again and looks about the room for a diversion. The top of the dresser is bare except for a lone photo frame lying on its face. Its posture hints that it has been deliberately turned over. She picks it up. It is a wedding photo. Her eyes lock onto the groom. His uniform is the khaki color of the armed forces, identical to that of the man in her dreams. She studies his features and compares them to her recollection of the newspaper photo. Robert's hairline was straighter, his eyebrows more arched, and his lips thinner, not full like the groom's.

A certainty swells within her. The soldier of her dreams is this groom, not the policeman in the newspaper. And the groom is a younger version of the man down the hall. It is not Robert Collier she has been seeking, but his father.

How can this be?

She studies the bride. A stranger. And yet...not. As she stares at the two of them arm-in-arm, another certainty announces itself: the only way to be free of the dreams and have a chance at a normal relationship is to confront what she feels for...Wil. Not Bill or William. *Wil.* The name sits in her consciousness like it has been there forever.

Still clutching the photo, she plunges into the hallway. The other bedroom door hangs open to darkness, but a faint light filters up the stairwell. She follows it down and finds him once more tending the stove.

His back stiffens and without turning around he says, "Ms. Pearson, I suggest you return to your room and stay there until morning."

"We have to talk, Wil."

He spins around. "What did you call me?" He looks at the photo in her hands and grabs it roughly from her, his eyes cold with anger. "What are you doing with this?"

A lock of hair has fallen onto his forehead. It feels like the most natural thing in the world for her to lift it up and

🌺 *Grey Area* 🌺

Revenant

slide it back into place. But her actions do not have the calming effect she has anticipated.

Instead, he jerks away, as if her fingers have burned him. "What the hell are you doing?"

"Please let me explain. For years I've had dreams about a man in uniform." She points to the photograph. "You are that man."

His features wrinkle in disbelief. "You said you came here looking for Rob!"

She takes one step closer; he takes two back.

"When I saw that newspaper photo of Robert, I confused him with you."

He inhales roughly. "You're not making any sense."

"You've visited my dreams since my early teens. Because of you, I haven't been able to have any kind of relationship with another man."

He shakes his head and tries to step back again, but the wall behind prevents it.

"Upstairs, when we were lying together, didn't you feel something?" She steps close and lays a hand on his heaving chest. "Don't you feel it now?"

He slides out of her grasp to the side. "Of course I feel something. I'm a middle-aged man for Chrissake, and you're a beautiful young woman."

"Do you love someone else then?" This might explain his reluctance.

"No." He studies the photo in his hands.

She edges a little closer. "How long ago did she die?"

He remains silent so long, she begins to fear he will never answer. Then, in a voice so low she has to strain to hear, he says, "It's been almost twenty-five years. We'd come up here for Christmas. She died trying to save a friend of Rob's who fell through the ice." His eyes return to her, sharpened with anger. "Before you were even born."

An image from childhood comes to Cassie. The first time she met her aunt, the woman had peered into Cassie's eyes as if looking into her soul and hissed, "You're not one of us!"

&a; Grey Area &a;

Nancy MacLean

She inhales sharply to bring back the present and looks up at Wil. "What about reincarnation? I'm almost twenty-five. Maybe I was your wife."

"That's insane!" His expression and tone reflect his disbelief.

"Oh, you can be so God-awful stubborn!" Despair rips through her. She is destined to be forever alone. She turns away to hide tears she cannot stop and heads toward stairs so familiar she knows she can navigate them in the dark.

Before she can mount the first step, a large hand grabs her right wrist. He slowly pulls her around to face him.

"Aileen...my wife...she—she used to tell me that...in those exact same words."

A memory drops into her mind. She responds, "And you would tell me I was as equally bull-headed."

Her words make the doubt in his features fade ever so slightly. She steps closer and this time he doesn't back away. She goes up onto her toes in an attempt to bring her face close to his, but two inches still separate their lips. After an unbearably long hesitation, he brings his mouth down to hers. His kiss is soft, gentle, the kiss of her dreams. She wants more and she can sense he does too.

He leans away and frowns down at her, but keeps his grip on her wrist. "None of this makes sense," he whispers.

"It doesn't have to. Let's not waste this moment." She takes his hand and turns to lead him up the stairs.

Again he tugs her back around. "Are you sure this is what you want?"

She is now on the first step and doesn't have to look up very high to peer into his eyes. "It is you I want, Wil Collier. You and no other."

His expression tells her he remembers these words too and he lifts her in his arms and carries her up the stairs and down the hall. As he lays her upon the bed, it all feels so familiar, yet excitingly new.

Later, when they are spent and breathless, they fill the remaining hours of the night talking about Robert. The man he is fishing with is the same childhood friend Aileen had saved before succumbing to the frigid waters twenty-five years before. Just before Cassie had been born. *Another life, another chance.* She breathes in contentment. If she hadn't seen Robert's picture in the paper, this miraculous reunion would never have happened.

This is one dream from which she does not want to awaken.

🙎

She blinks away the fog of sleep. Grey light lingers beyond a window rattled by a wind now dry of rain. She is cold, so very cold. *Where is Wil?* She flies down the stairs and sees a note on the table:

Couldn't find your clothes. Went to get more from your car.

She looks down. She is wearing her windbreaker and jeans. Why would he be looking for them? She steps outside to see him stumbling toward her, his shoulders stooped, his face distorted with grief.

When he sees her, he holds up a hand. "No! Don't go down there!"

But she has to see what bothers him so. She pushes through him and down the driveway, the journey that had seemed so arduous the night before now effortless.

The car's lone headlamp no longer shines. Next to the tree, within the crumpled side of the car, she sees a slumped form. A small form wearing a blue windbreaker. She looks down at herself, but sees nothing. She holds her hands in front of her face but they are not there.

"Aileen, don't leave!" His words are rough, as if forced through a burning throat. He staggers to the car and collapses onto his knees. As he buries his face in his hands, his shoulders shake with a long-borne grief. She hovers above, desperately wanting to comfort him.

🙎 *Grey Area* 🙎

Nancy MacLean

"Dad?" A young man climbs out of a mud-splattered truck, his left arm in a sling. Her son, Robert. No longer a child, but a man. Years of hugging him, holding him, taken from her now as it had been taken from her then.

Wil clambers to his feet and wipes his eyes with the sleeves of his coat. Robert slowly approaches the car and then reaches inside to the still form. After a moment, he straightens up and looks back at his father. "How long has she been here?"

"Since..." Wil pauses, clears his throat and then begins again, "since last night."

"I didn't even know you were here. Just thought I'd check on the place before I headed back to Halifax." He looks from the car to his father. "So you knew her, then?"

Wil's nod is brief.

Robert gently pulls on his father's arm. "Come on, Dad. Let's go down to the village."

With a heavy step, Wil follows his son to the truck. Before getting in, he pauses and looks first at the mangled car, then at the surrounding trees, and finally up at the sky. He is looking for her.

She wants to tell him that she is okay, that they will see each other again, somewhere, somehow. But the time for words has passed.

She summons what remains of her scattering energy and, with the help of the wind, gently lifts a lock of hair that has fallen onto his forehead. He inhales sharply. Then his bottom lip begins to quiver.

"Dad? Are you okay?" Robert says from the other side of the truck, his eyes, so like his father's, dark with worry.

After a long, shaky breath, Wil looks at his son.

"Yeah," he says, with a trace of a smile. "I am."

𐐚 Grey Area 𐐚

Revenant

NANCY MACLEAN is a retired physical therapist whose passions include writing, ice hockey, and playing the drums. Hailing from Moncton, New Brunswick, she has lived in Calgary, Houston, and Toronto before moving to the Halifax region in 2006. Since pursuing writing in 1989 she has belonged to writing groups in each of these cities, and served one year as president of the Woodlands Writers Guild in Houston, Texas. Her novel *MAD (Mutually Assured Destruction)* won the 2000 Authorlink Award for Science Fiction. Her fascination with the paranormal weaves a thread in most of her novels and short stories.

Mildred Mudd's Epiphany

Charlotte Musial

Mildred Mudd creeps about her kitchen this frigid February morning while heating water for coffee and waiting for her friend, Bridget, to arrive. She can still feel the shape of the phone in her trembling hand as she'd called Bridget twenty minutes ago, and fragments of their conversation float in her agitated mind, right alongside orders to herself to 'get a grip.'

"...must come immediately..." she'd begun.

"...can't, Mil. Look out...ice storm...break a leg if..."

"...do it for you if..."

"Tell me..."

"...can't on the phone..."

For another twenty minutes after hanging up, Mildred paces from window to window, oblivious to the ice-encased landscape over which Bridget—frail, breakable Bridget—must navigate to reach the modest, going-to-ruin bungalow in which Mildred has peacefully, if dully, lived her long widowhood.

It was a dream, she tells herself. *Had to be a dream. Foolish me. What am I doing, dragging dear Bridget out of bed to tell her about it? How silly.* She picks up the phone to call her friend back, but Bridget's phone rings and rings. *Too late.*

Charlotte Musial

Nothing to do now but hope Bridget doesn't break any bones on her journey.

Mildred resumes pacing while memories of last night's dream preempt images of the outside crystalline world. She sees again the...thing...she has no other word for it...at the foot of her bed. And yet, 'thing' seems an obscene word because, she has to admit, it was beautiful. More than beautiful: exquisite.

But eerie. A child. A girl child. Wrapped in filmy fabric, or mist, or...an aura. A halo. Something. Wisps of undulating light and a shimmer of silvery hair. The child's right hand clasped the diaphanous robe in front, as though to prevent tripping; her left hand rose aloft as if to command Mildred's attention. And most eerie of all, her eyes, large, luminous grey, fringed with velvety dark lashes.

"I'm Holly," the child whispered. But *didn't* whisper, because her lips didn't move. Still, Mildred heard the words. In the next instant, the child vanished.

Shaken, Mildred fumbled in the dark for her bedside lamp. The old tick-tock clock on the table beside it showed 3:00am.

She lay awake, tense and troubled, until dawn, going over and over the experience. Then she finally arose, called Bridget, and began pacing.

Unable to stop herself, Mildred dials Bridget again, imagining her leaving her small apartment, hearing the phone ring and ring while debating whether to turn back and answer it. But she's already halfway down the icy, outside stairs and can't face the return journey for what she suspects can only be Mildred again, urging her to hurry.

Now there's a puzzle, Bridget must be thinking. *Staid, stolid Mildred, sounding like she's in a panic.* Never, in all the years they'd been friends, had this happened! *Mildred, who never fails to find a rational explanation for anything, sounding almost...irrational.*

Mildred visualizes Bridget treading carefully over slippery sidewalks, trying to rush without falling, using her arms like miniature windmills for balance. Her eyes searching

🐌 Grey Area 🐌

out bare patches on the pavement to place her boots before proceeding to the next oasis, propelled by a growing sense of urgency.

Mildred is thankful that it's still early and traffic is light. Bridget can pick her way across the street of the quiet neighbourhood and find shelter from the harbour's gale among the old buildings of the North End.

⚉

Still wearing her housecoat, hair screwed into a frizzy bed-head, Mildred opens her front door to a blast of freezing air and a red-faced Bridget, whose own hair straggles outside her scarlet tuque into icicles formed by the freezing of her breath.

"I tried to call you back to say I was okay and not to bother," Mildred says before Bridget can utter a word. "But you didn't answer."

"You're *okay*?" Bridget peers at Mildred's face, as pock-marked as an orange peel and as pale, now, as pearls. "So how come you look like you just saw a ghost?"

Mildred recoils. "You know I don't believe in ghosts."

"A manner of speaking," Bridget says, prying off her boots. "That coffee sure smells good." She follows Mildred from the front door through the hall and into the kitchen. "Any muffins? To go with it?"

"Don't I always?"

Mildred, whose single culinary triumph is muffins—any kind—opens her freezer door. "Banana? Cornmeal? Bran?" She feels desperate to instill normalcy into this unprecedented morning event.

"Banana. And cornmeal. One of each'd be good." Bridget perches on a kitchen chair, tucks one tiny foot beneath her bony bum, lets the other foot dangle. "Now," she says, as Mildred pops four muffins into the microwave oven to warm, "what's this all about? You sounded really spooked on the phone. What's up?"

Braced by the aroma of the coffee and by Bridget's company, Mildred shrugs. "Sorry," she says casually. "False alarm. Guess I just had a rough night." Eyeing Bridget's skeptical expression, she adds, "You know. Bad dreams." The microwave pings, and Mildred, literally feeling saved by the bell, springs to retrieve the muffins. "I'm sorry to have dragged you out so early. Thanks for coming, dear." Placing hot coffee, warm muffins, and butter before her friend, she says, "And what's new with you? Any good news from Noelle yet?" Noelle is Bridget's daughter who, every month, reports to her mom the current state of her fertility.

"Don't you dare pull that on me, Mildred Mudd. I know something happened. Think you can fool me after all this time? Huh!" Bridget pauses with her coffee mug halfway to her lips, butter melting on a morsel of warm banana muffin in her other hand. "Not likely! So, out with it." She pops the mealy morsel into her mouth. "And sit," she orders.

Mildred stops dithering and sits. She never could fool Bridget, no point trying. Bridget is on a mission now, and nothing will deter her. Resigned, Mildred stares mutely at her friend.

"Well?" Bridget prompts.

Mildred blushes. "I think I *did* see a ghost last night."

Bridget sputters and stifles a gasp. "Hello?"

Mildred knows that she is as likely to utter such words as Bridget is apt to quote James Joyce. No wonder her friend gasps.

"It was probably just a dream. But it spoke and woke me up. Or," Mildred shrugs again, "I woke up and then it spoke. I'm not sure." Her voice trails off. "Really startled me." She rises and tops up their mugs. "But I figure now it *was* just a really vivid dream, and that's why I tried to call you back to say don't bother coming. I mean," she adds, realizing how tactless she sounds, "if you didn't want to. Since it's so cold out. And slippery."

"Well, I'm here now, so you might as well tell me all about it." Bridget returns to her muffin. She adds another

Mildred Mudd's Epiphany

generous blob of butter to its warm interior. "Starting with what this mysterious 'it' is."

Mildred hesitates, then she says, "A child. Girl. A beautiful little girl."

"And?" Bridget stares, her dark eyes wide and round in her elfin face. "There must be more. Like, beautiful how? And what exactly did she say?"

Might as well come clean, Mildred thinks. *There'll be no peace until I do.* Still trying to appear nonchalant, she describes the scene that awakened her at three o'clock.

For Bridget, any suggestion of the supernatural is the staff of life. Rapt, she listens until Mildred finishes. Then she says, "And she said her name was 'Holly?'"

"Right."

"Who's Holly?"

"I've no idea. Never knew anybody by that name." Mildred begins to fuss with clearing the table of cups and crumbs. "Go figure."

"But Mil, there must be some connection..." Bridget thinks for a moment and then asks, "Do you like it?"

"Like what?"

"The name. Holly."

Mildred, who intensely dislikes her own name, says, "Yes, I suppose I do."

"Why?"

Knowing Bridget won't let her dismiss the question, Mildred smothers her irritation. "You know I don't dwell on things like that, Bridget. But, if I *had* to say (*and it appears I do,* she adds *sotto voce*)...I'd say it brings to mind thoughts of holy, and maybe...halo. I just like the sound of it."

"It must be significant in some way."

"None I can think of."

"Tell me again what she looked like."

Halfway through her description this time, Mildred halts and sucks in a big breath, eyes wide and unfocused.

"What?" Bridget demands.

"My God, I just remembered. Her eyes!"

"What about them?"

🍃 *Grey Area* 🍃

Mildred's gaze comes back to her friend, whose own eyes are wide with curiosity. "You're looking at them."

Bridget's mouth falls open. "You mean...?"

"They were *exactly* like my own. Like looking in a mirror." Then, "Just the eyes," she adds, aware that she couldn't have described the child as beautiful had that child otherwise resembled herself.

Electrified, Bridget whispers, "Could she be you, Mil? The *young* you?"

"No."

"How can you be sure?"

"She was beautiful. I never was."

"Oh, nonsense." Bridget sips her coffee. "Who, then?"

"I haven't a clue. Not a clue."

For a moment, both women are silent. Then Bridget, glancing at the clock, leaps from her chair. "I have to go, Mil. Noelle promised to call me this morning to let me know if I'm gonna be a grandma anytime soon. I'll call you; we have to get to the bottom of this mystery. Will you be okay alone?"

"Oh, mystery-pistery. Stop fussing. I've been okay alone for forty years. It was just a stupid dream."

I hope, she thinks, as she stands at the window and watches Bridget rush, in a restrained way, down the street and toward her home.

🙎

Mildred can't concentrate on the evening news. She spent the day cleaning the cupboards, the oven, and the fridge. She mopped the kitchen floor. She read the daily paper from front to back, including the sports and business sections, pinning her attention to the pages by sheer will. She wrote cheques and filed receipts. Then she prepared and ate a light supper—a tuna sandwich and a small, green salad. Then, exhausted, she took a hot bath and settled in front of the TV with a glass of wine.

Mildred Mudd's Epiphany

And the whole time, anxiety, like a mouse, gnawed at the edge of her mind.

Finally, when she can no longer even pretend to follow the ER plot, she turns off the TV, checks that the doors are locked, and gets ready for bed.

As she smoothes moisture cream on her face, a long-buried memory arises. It's of Ben and the evening of their fifth anniversary. He'd crept up behind her as she was creaming her face. He lifted her hair and nibbled the nape of her neck, a gesture that would on other occasions have either melted her bones or reduced her to giggles, depending on her mood. But on this night, his gesture fell flat.

Surprised, Ben glanced at her pale reflection in the mirror, turned her around to face him, and asked what was wrong. She managed to convince him that she was just tired after a day digging in the garden, and after she'd hastily manufactured some details, he seemed to believe her.

They'd gone to bed then, and he'd fallen asleep cuddling her, while she'd lain awake, stifling sobs that drenched her pillow.

How could she have said it?

"Ben, I was saving my news for a surprise, until I was sure." *But today...today...*

Today, she'd been ironing Ben's shirt, just hours after her visit to the doctor. "June," he'd said. "Middle of June, you'll be a mom. No mistake this time."

His words echoed in her mind when the first pain struck, a bolt that buckled her body and caused her to fall forward against the ironing board for support. A second spasm immediately grabbed her, drove her to the floor on her knees. There she remained, suspended, dimly aware of the October sunshine outside the window and, from the schoolyard across the street, children's voices. She could never say, afterwards, what roused her first, the smell of scorching cloth above her head or the sensation of hot wetness between her thighs. Trembling, using the legs of the ironing board for leverage, she'd pulled herself up, unplugged the iron, and fumbled for the charred, half-ironed shirt.

🍃 Grey Area 🍃

Charlotte Musial

With the next pain, blood gushed down her legs, into her shoes, and onto the floor. With Ben's shirt pressed between her thighs, she staggered to the bathroom. She knew it was over, knew with primitive certainty that she'd lost their baby daughter.

A few hours later, weak and shaky, but no longer hemorrhaging, she went to the woodshed and extricated a shovel from the tangle of tools stored there. She carried it to the perennial bed and, summoning her strength, she half-turned, half-scraped four shovels full of soil, and in that small hollow close to the lilac bush, she laid Ben's shirt, stained with the remains of her pregnancy.

Two years later, Ben died of pneumonia and went to his grave never knowing that he'd almost been a father.

From that day to this, Mildred had never told anyone about their loss. She'd mourned; God knew, she'd mourned. But she hadn't told Ben.

Her doctor knew, of course, but no one else.

Now, for the first time, looking at herself in the mirror, Mildred seriously asks herself why. Had she felt it a personal failure? Were the words just too difficult to say? Would voicing the loss have made it too real? But she has no answers.

Mildred recaps the moisture cream and goes to bed.

She falls asleep quickly.

For three more nights she sleeps soundly.

On the fourth night, the child reappears.

Tell someone. So I can come again.

Mildred bolts up in bed, but the visitor has already vanished, leaving Mildred rattled and clutching her heart. She arises, and remains anxious and distracted all that day, glancing over her shoulder, pausing to listen for some message from the spheres, the spheres she doesn't believe in.

A week later, when she's begun to relax again, the plea to *tell someone* reaches a new pitch of intensity, jolting Mildred out of a deep, dreamless slumber and bouncing around her room as if released in an echo chamber.

Anger banishes her panic. "Tell what?" she demands.

You know.

✻ Grey Area ✻

Mildred Mudd's Epiphany

A cloud of light shimmers at the foot of the bed and then dissipates.

When Mildred and Bridget next meet in town for coffee, Mildred relates the latest development.

"And that's it?" Bridget says when she finishes. "'Tell someone' and 'you know'? That's all she said?" Bridget stares through Tim Horton's window into the parking lot where mud, dirt and grease lay like sin on the snow, while rivulets of water escape from under the grungy banks in a sudden thaw.

Mildred swirls cappuccino in her nearly empty cup and fiddles with the last of her bagel and cream cheese. "That's it."

"Hmm," Bridget says. "Back in a sec." And she is, with a second cup of coffee and a blueberry muffin, ready to do battle.

"That's *every* word she said? No hint of what it is you're supposed to tell? Or who you're supposed to tell it to? Or why?" Bridget's eyes skewer Mildred.

Mildred fidgets. "Oh, for Pete's sake," she says, annoyed. "If you *must* know, she also said, '*So I can come back again.*'"

Bridget gasps. "Mildred! That's the answer! This little soul is in limbo and is trying to get out! Don't you see? You're her way back into the world!" Bridget crackles with excitement. "That's why she's telling you to..." Bridget stops. She swallows. "Why you? Why you, of all people?"

"Darned if I know." Mildred leans back in her chair and watches cars line up in the drive-through. "And I've already told you about her. I don't know what else I'm supposed to do."

Bridget rolls her eyes. "You have to be the most obtuse person I've ever known, Mildred Mudd. You're enough to drive a person crazy." She pushes her muffin aside, springs from her chair and, to the other coffee drinkers' amusement, paces the floor. Then, smacking her forehead and uttering oaths, she returns to reclaim her seat.

Charlotte Musial

Mildred sits at the table, impervious to Bridget's antics or their audience. "What's the news from Noelle?" she asks, before Bridget can speak.

"Same," she replies. Then, "Let's go." She grabs her purse from the table and bursts out the door of the coffee shop.

Mildred remains seated.

Bridget retraces her steps and finds Mildred motionless, gazing into space. She sits again and stares at her friend. When a few moments pass without any sign that Mildred is aware of her presence, she says, "Earth to Mil. Are you there, dear?"

Mildred resurfaces. But still she doesn't speak.

"What is it? You look like you've seen a gh—" Bridget stops. "You remember something, don't you?"

Mildred swallows. "There's only one thing in my life worth telling that I've never told anyone. Not *anyone*."

Bridget reaches across the table and covers Mildred's hand with her own.

"When Ben and I were married for five years, I lost a baby. I couldn't tell him. We'd been hoping so much for so long...right from the start, really." Mildred's eyes fill with tears. "I've always believed the baby was a girl." She tries not to blink. "I never got pregnant again, and two years later, Ben died. He never knew." She reaches for the tissue that Bridget discreetly offers and dabs at her tears before they fall. "I couldn't talk about it. I thought that if I didn't talk about it, maybe...maybe it didn't really happen."

"I know what that's like. I truly do. And I'm so sorry. I'm glad you told me. It will be one of our secrets, I promise. No one will ever hear it from me. Not your secret, and not one word of your dream." She releases Mildred's hand and angles her own body as if to shield her friend from the curious gazes of others in the coffee shop.

"Do you think," Bridget says cautiously, "that maybe Holly needs your permission to...to come again to someone close to you? Someone who loves you as she would've? As she still apparently must?"

⚜ Grey Area ⚜

Mildred Mudd's Epiphany

For a moment Mildred is silent. Then she says, "Well, if it's my permission she needs, Bridge, she has it."

They gather their belongings and leave the shop.

With a quick hug, they separate at Mildred's front door. "I'll call you," Bridget says. "We'll have coffee at my place in a few days, okay?"

"Okay. And, thanks. For everything."

As winter wanes, Mildred sleeps at night undisturbed. She's relieved to be free of her little nighttime visitor, but wonders, occasionally, if telling Bridget the story of her lost baby has anything to do with the dream-girl's absence. She resumes her solitary life, interrupted only by regular visits with Bridget and by a new and unaccustomed sense of peace.

April arrives and with it, hints of spring. Mildred thinks briefly, as she and Bridget walk home from Easter Mass, of the early days when she so looked forward to seeing her tulip and daffodils poke their tiny green spears through the dark soil into the light and air. She wonders if she could garden again. Maybe dig a little in the back yard this fall, start really small, bury a few bulbs with their papery skins and wait for their springtime magic.

"You're quiet," Bridget says.

"Just thinking." Mildred pauses. "The lilies on the altar were nice, weren't they?"

"Lovely. New life every spring. Or maybe," Bridget adds softly, "old life renewed."

"What do you mean?"

"Well, you know. In nature. Everything seems to die, but doesn't. Take trees, for example. Every winter you'd swear they were dead. And every spring, presto! Alive again."

"Yes. But even trees eventually *do* die." Mildred's tone implies 'end of story.'

"They do. You're right about that."

"Well?"

Charlotte Musial

"I like to think about what happens next."

"Which is?"

"You tell me, Mil."

They stroll in silence for a few blocks, Bridget as silent now as her companion was earlier. Mildred ponders Bridget's last comment, senses, as Bridget opens the door to her apartment, that she has something to tell her, something she's holding back.

Halfway through a lunch of potato salad, ham, and a fresh roll in Bridget's kitchen, Mildred says. "The trees."

"Hmm?" Bridget still seems preoccupied. "What about the trees?"

"You said. What comes next. After they die."

"Yes?"

"The little maple tree Ben and I planted the first year we were married? It grew and grew and grew, and then one spring, it just didn't. Not a leaf, not a bud. I cried." Mildred blushes. "It so reminded me of Ben. Of our hopes for the future."

Bridget puts down her fork and stares at Mildred. "Yes?"

"A few years later—Ben was dead a long time by then—four new maples sprang up all around the poor old trunk. Was I surprised! It was almost like it was having babies." Mildred grabs her napkin and uses it to hide her face. "Listen to me. I'm getting old and foolish."

"You think?" Bridget asks quietly.

Mildred isn't finished. "But here's the oddest thing. The next year, I discovered, yards and yards away from the old tree, another one! All by itself, against the farthest fence." She begins to eat again. "And that's the biggest one of all now. Must be eight feet tall."

Bridget nods, and they return to their lunch.

"Well?" Mildred says. "I know something's on your mind. Out with it."

"You'll never guess. Never, never!"

Only one thing could cause this euphoria in Bridget's face and voice, but Mildred bites her tongue and waits, allowing Bridget the pleasure of relating her news in her own

Mildred Mudd's Epiphany

time. She waits some more while coffee is poured and meringues served on small blue plates alongside cheery, left-over Valentine napkins and a blue butter dish.

Finally, Bridget settles. Mildred sips her coffee and smiles. "Well, out with it," she says again.

Bridget raises her cup and tilts it in Mildred's direction. "You may offer me a toast. I'm going to be a grandma!"

"No!"

"Yes! Noelle called me last night. We're going to have a Christmas baby! *Another* Christmas baby, just like Noelle herself!"

"Congratulations! That's wonderful news. I'm thrilled for you." Mildred scoops up a meringue and piles it with strawberry jam. "I suppose it's too early to tell if it's a boy or a girl?"

"I think it is. And anyway, they don't want to know." Bridget crumples her napkin. "They want to be surprised."

"I can understand that." About to add that *she* wouldn't want to know either, Mildred remembers with a pang that, without the benefit of science, she *had* known.

She also knows that Bridget is still holding something back.

"They've already picked out names." Bridget fidgets some more, this time with her cup and saucer.

"And?"

"Christopher for a boy."

"I love it!" Mildred says. "And for a girl?" Mildred raises her meringue to her lips, holds it there and waits. Holds it and waits.

"Would you believe...Holly?" Bridget smiles.

Mildred slowly lowers her meringue.

"Holly," she whispers. She reaches for Bridget's hand. "Holly."

And in that moment, Mildred feels something she hasn't felt since that morning so long ago when the doctor said, "You're going to be a mom." Mildred feels light. She feels beautiful. She feels free.

Charlotte Musial

Although CHARLOTTE MUSIAL believes that much of life falls into the 'grey area,' "Mildred Mudd's Epiphany" is her first venture into the speculative literature genre. Her publication credits include short fiction in *The Cape Breton County Monitor, The Atlantic Advocate,* and *The Nashwaak Review.* Her entry in *Canadian Writer's Journal* short story competition (2011) received honourable mention. Two short stories are scheduled to appear in an upcoming anthology by Boularderie Island Press. Her poetry has appeared in *Pottersfield Portfolio* and *Inner Visions, Outer Voices: An Anthology of Cape Breton Poetry* published by UCCB Press (1988), and her personal essays and short memoirs have found homes in *The Cape Bretoner, The Globe and Mail, National Post,* and on CBC Radio One, "First Person Singular." In 2013, "An Accidental Pas de Deux," an account of life with her husband, Maurice Currie and Parkinson's Disease, was long listed in the Canada Writes competition, creative nonfiction category. She is a long-time member of Writers' Federation of Nova Scotia, a charter member of Douglas Arthur Brown's master-class workshops, and a creative affiliate of Access Copyright. She lives in Sydney.

My Mews

Nancy S.M. Waldman

"Aly, come for a walk."

"No. It's cold. Frankly, I'd rather die."

Sara, my best friend, greeted this bit of black humour with a stony silence. She did not find my jokes about death funny and I knew it.

My husband Neal died five and a half months ago. A drunken limousine driver lurched over a curb and ran him down. After a ridiculously rapid and large settlement from their insurance company, I quit my copy editing job. Sara cursed the money, saying that if I had to get out in the world and do something every day, I'd be further along, less depressed, more recovered.

I needed her, but her demands for my recovery grated on me.

Ushering her out with many reassurances, I locked the door and crawled into bed, noticing as I went down the hallway that the light—the one I kept on all the time since Neal's death—was off.

Sara. Dammit. Stop being my mother and father all rolled into one. I got up, padded over in my sock feet and yanked on the chain, flicking it back on.

Nancy S.M. Waldman

&

The day Neal and I planned to put a deposit on a different apartment—one that was okay, but not what we'd hoped for—Neal texted me: *Apt. Come see.*

He GPS'd me the location. Tremont Heights, only the city's most perfect neighbourhood. The one with trees and cool people and dogs and parks and sidewalk cafes and friendly bars. He also sent a photo of a hand-painted sign in front of a grand old house. It read, "Apt. Good condition."

"Hmm," I said to myself, "must be a dump."

But it wasn't. Neal happened to arrive on this street in this neighbourhood on the exact morning that the lovely Mrs. Denitch, who didn't own a computer and had never heard of Craig's List, had put out her For Rent sign.

The century-old, restored, garage apartment (Mrs. Denitch called it a "mews") became our home. Perfect, with one bedroom, one bath, a galley kitchen and living/dining room, it also had wood floors, twelve-inch plaster moldings around twelve-foot ceilings, arched doorways, built-in shelving and drawers, vintage light fixtures, huge windows, and French doors that led to a balcony overlooking Mrs. Denitch's back yard shaded with giant oaks. Plus, a window seat in the kitchen.

Neal and I lived here together long enough to paint the living room eggplant, the bedroom heather, the bathroom robin's egg blue and the kitchen shabby chic white with blue and butter yellow accents. We couldn't believe our fortune.

Sara wants me to leave the apartment. She really doesn't get it.

&

I slept till early evening. On my way to the bathroom I noticed that the light had blinked off again.

The bulb must have finally burned out.

& Grey Area &

My Mews

I climbed into the shower and immediately started crying.

To amuse myself, I've made up words for different kinds of tears. I felt the need for differentiation for the same reason, I assume, that the Inuit have fifty words for snow. Some tears sting. Some cleanse. Some make you feel lighter, some heavier. Some wash away worries. Most don't.

Crying in the shower: *Crynsing*. Crying while cooking a meal that you will eat by yourself: *Crief*, which is spelled like "grief," but pronounced like "chef." Tears, after drinking too much, while too alone: *Swallow*. Tears while cleaning: *Sweeping*. A crying jag that makes you feel better, however briefly: *Crycovery*. Bawling that sends you to the floor in a helpless puddle: *Cryptonite*.

🐾

Darkness had overtaken the apartment when I came out. The light from the bathroom cut an elongated V of brightness down the short hallway to the living room. The sharpness of the light/dark line unnerved me. Death, the sharpest edge of all, will do that to a person. As I passed the wall sconce, I automatically reached up and yanked the chain.

The light came on.

That bulb's supposed to be burned out— Holy shit!

I sprinted into the living room, turning on lights as I went. Once the rooms were bathed in incandescence, I started breathing again, though too rapidly. I made myself slow it down. *I can't afford to get spooked. I live alone. I live here alone. This is my home. I have to hold it together.*

I turned on the radio.

*What the hell is going on with that light? The chain has to be pulled for it to go off or on. I turned it on before going to sleep. It was off when I got up. Now it's on again. If the bulb's not out...*I looked at it from my self-appointed safe spot on the living room couch...*then someone—somebody—had to pull the chain to turn it off.*

🐾 Grey Area 🐾

Nancy S.M. Waldman

It wasn't the first spooky thing that had happened.

I called Sara, more to hear a human voice than for information, but I had to ask. "Did you turn off the light in my hallway when you were here?"

"Uh, I don't know. Why?"

"It's not a light switch. It's that wall sconce with the chain. In the hallway. Did you turn it off?"

"No. Definitely not. Why?"

"It keeps flipping off. I'm freaked out by it."

"Talk to the landlady."

"Talking to the landlady about electricity is the husband's job," I said, tearing up.

"Aly..."

"I know. I know."

After hanging up I wondered if Sara could be playing tricks on me so that I'd move, like what Jimmy Stewart did to Ingrid Bergman in *Gaslight*. But I knew that was stupid. Sara's trying to get me sane, not drive me crazy.

⚉

Objects moved around the apartment, seemingly of their own volition. But that was more irritating than spooky and my shoddy housekeeping and colander-like memory were ready and convenient excuses to explain these incidents away.

A week or so after the hallway light scare, I walked into the kitchen and saw a hard-edged shadow, like the flight of a large bird on a sunny day, passing over the window seat at the end of the room.

An involuntary and very odd *erking* noise came out of my throat. *What the hell was that?* My eyes playing tricks on me? Or something that caught the light?

I stood, shaky, immobile. There were no dangling things. No chandelier pieces. No ceiling fan blades. *What about one of the knives that hung on the back splash? That's it. One of them reflected the light when I turned it on and...Oh Jesus. No. It wasn't light, but dark. A shadow.*

⚉ Grey Area ⚉

My Mews

Suddenly, I couldn't stand still. I ran to the bedroom and pulled the covers over my head.

Neal, damn you! Why aren't you with me?

Hello, Anger. I see you've returned.

The stages of grief were now as familiar to me as food groups or multiplication tables. I bashed back and forth between anger and depression about forty times a day. No wonder I had to sleep all the time. All that bashing.

And then a tiny thought interrupted the wash of anger. *What if Neal* is *with me? What if he's trying to send me a message?*

Hope, this hope anyway, felt like an icy trickle down my spine. I wanted it to be Neal—of course I did—but if it were, wouldn't I feel warmth? Sweetness? Love, instead of fear? Wouldn't I know? Otherwise, what's the point? I lay in our bed, eyes wide, muscles strained, straight and tense.

The apartment might as well be your tomb, Aly. No wonder there's a ghost.

&

I talked myself down. If someone were in the apartment, they would have long since come in and hacked me to pieces, or worse. I had to get up, eat and watch TV all night.

I snatched my laptop from the dresser where it had been recharging. The battery was kaput. At the very least, I should get a longer extension cord. Buying a new battery. Buying an extension cord. Just two of the things I neglected to do every day. Like talk to Mrs. Denitch about the light. But I could put that off because it seemed to be fine now. It shone brightly as I went to the kitchen.

Later, when Sara called to check on me, I was feeling pretty good. "You'll be happy to know that I'm making a list of things I need to take care of," I told her. I almost mentioned the spooky shadow, but thought better of it. No need to give her ammunition. Instead, I blabbed on and on, needing human contact.

Nancy S.M. Waldman

"Did you ever think about the fact that the word apartment contains the word 'apart'?" I asked her.

"No, I never did."

"Why is it called an apartment? Shouldn't it be compartment? Or, department? No, that should be a train station."

"Aly, I know you love words, but this is ridiculous. You need something productive to occupy your mind."

Objectively, I knew Sara was right about me needing to leave, to move on. She was right about everything.

But who lives their life objectively?

To-Do List
Battery
Extension Cord
Clean out fridge
Buy light bulbs
Clean bathroom
Clean everything
Talk to landlady?
Job?
Start that blog
Yoga class?
Get a dog?
WRITE SOMETHING
Kill myself...hahahaha Joke!

It is a joke. I would never commit suicide. Who would remember Neal if I weren't around? No. I am a witness to his having been alive. To the great and wonderful person he was. I am not going anywhere. I can't be happy, but I can go on.

So, I joke.

My Mews

The light started doing its thing again, so I made myself go looking for the adorable Mrs. Denitch. I found in her in the front yard and explained the problem.

"Oh dear," she said, taking off gardening gloves that somehow looked elegant on her, "we can't have that. I'll call the electrician. You know the whole place was re-wired. But I supposed these things can happen. Have you had any problem with mice?"

"I don't think so." *Maybe I had. Could mice move car keys?* "Mrs. Denitch, do you know the history of this place?"

"Of course, it's been in my family since it was built."

"Have a lot of people lived in my apartment?"

"Not really. I only started renting it after the renovation. That was five or six years ago. You and your husband—" she stopped and looked up at me apologetically. I nodded her on, so she finished. "You're the third renters. People seem to like it."

Would others like it if it were haunted?

"What about before that?"

"Vacant for decades. The structure was originally a stable and carriage house. The stableman lived upstairs."

"Oh my, that was a long time ago."

She nodded eagerly. "I remember him vividly. Holman Taylor. He was quite the striking figure of a man."

"How long ago are we talking about?"

"Late '20s, I'd say. We had a lot of property back then. Long after everyone switched over to automobiles, we kept the horses. They were more pets than transportation, but my father retained Holman to look after them. He had such a handsome face. What do they call it? Chiseled?"

I smiled at her. "Like Clark Gable?"

She grinned back. "No, Clark was soft compared to Holman. More like that Matthew—what's his name?—from the romantic comedies. The one with all the muscles and the Texas accent."

"McConaughey."

"He's the one."

Nancy S.M. Waldman

We laughed together and I wondered why it had taken me so long to come see her.

"The stableman wore old-fashioned clothes. I mean, even for then. He was a relic. How could a romantic little girl like me ever forget him?"

"So after he died, the place was vacant?"

"Uh-huh, until we decided to fix up everything." Her brow wrinkled and she reached out, placing a cool, dry hand on my forearm. "Do you know yet what you're going to do? Are you going to stay?"

I, of course, burst into tears. The someone-is-being-unexpectedly-tender-with-you crying jag comes on as fast as a sneeze. I called it *The Gusher*.

Mrs. Denitch's brow creases grew much deeper. She whipped a tissue from the wrist band of her sweater and handed it to me. "I understand a little bit, dear. I lost my husband. Of course, he wasn't so young. And neither was I."

I nodded. "But you were used to having him around," I said, my voice wavering weirdly. "And it's hard to sleep alone. I'm sure you do understand."

"I wish I could help."

"I know. I just..." We looked at each other for a long moment. "I want to stay in the apartment."

Her brow wrinkles disappeared with the onset of the warmest smile I could remember ever having directed at me. "I'm going to call the electrician right now."

I woke in the middle of the night choking, gasping, disoriented. I sat up on the couch where I'd fallen asleep, my hand over my pounding heart.

I've been smote, I thought, still in my dream.

Smote. Nice word, Aly.

Then, thunder-lightning came simultaneously. All the lights were off. The TV black and silent. The laptop lifeless. I tapped the space bar. Nothing. *Damned battery.*

My Mews

I sat back, trying to clear my head, to calm my heart. I wanted to close my eyes and sleep through the inky blackness, but adrenaline had flooded my brain. On high alert, my chest and shoulders felt tight and light like I'd just finished a sprint. My thoughts bounced. Ping-Pong balls inside my skull.

Neal loved thunderstorms. I wish we'd gotten a dog. I could comfort him. Her. It. We should have gotten a dog. But we couldn't agree on what kind. How old? Purebred or mutt? We kept not doing it. Get one now? What's the point? Someone to care for. Company. Noise. Someone to go for a walk with. Someone to be more scared of thunder than you are. Someone to sleep with.

Tears filled my eyes, but I recognized them as minor annoyance tears. They wouldn't develop into a good cry. They stung. Hurting, whiny tears. *Snivlets*, I finally decided, wishing I could type it onto the list on my computer.

I might start a blog of my lexicon. It's on my to-do list. Other people out there are grieving, too.

The electricity flickered on, then off again. I looked up, hopeful, and in the moment it took for that flicker—on and off, just that long—I beheld an ivory figure of a man like a statue, regal and formal, standing in the arched doorway between the kitchen and the living room. His left arm stretched out to the side, pointing toward the hallway.

In the next instant, there was only darkness, and me, wishing for a Rottweiler.

I raced to the bedroom. As I got to the hallway, my toe bashed up against something hard and I tumbled forward, hitting my knee on the floor. *What the hell?* I felt around and my hands found a large, hardcover book.

A book? I was a bad housekeeper, but even I wouldn't leave a book in the hallway. Besides the fact that I hadn't read anything since Neal died.

I struggled to my feet with the book under my arm and limped-ran to the bed where I covered my head and stayed awake in terror until the lights finally came back on two hours later.

Nancy S.M. Waldman

I passed the time wondering if this could be Neal trying, in some lame and round-about way, to contact me. I knew one thing: that hadn't been Neal standing in the living room. *Too tall, too...statue-y. Holman?* That made no sense. *Why would some other dead man come back to let me know that Neal was still with me? Why wouldn't Neal put in an appearance?*

If Neal *was* responsible, his communication abilities hadn't improved with death. I definitely wasn't getting the message.

&

My cell phone woke me.

"Aly? It's Mrs. Denitch. The electrician is here. I sent her back. Just wanted to warn you."

"Thanks. Talk to you later," I said, already halfway to the bathroom. By the time I had peed and splashed water on my face, there was a knock.

Good thing you sleep in your clothes, Aly.

I opened the door and launched into a rather insulting chat with the electrician about how surprising it was to see a woman in the role. She took it good-naturedly considering she must have heard it from every customer every day of her career. I finally shut up and showed her the fixture. She went to work, leaving the door open and going downstairs several times.

I went to the bedroom, thinking about the night before.

Had it been real? I pulled up my pants leg and saw a deep blue bruise on my left knee. That wasn't a dream, which meant I couldn't have dreamed the book either.

The book! Where is it?

I looked through the rumpled, filthy sheets. Nothing. It wasn't on the bedside table. I threw myself across the bed and saw it on the floor. Scrunching forward, I picked it up. Pulling back on the bed and wiggling up against the headboard, I adjusted the pillows and turned the book over.

The Care and Feeding of the Soul.

& Grey Area &

My Mews

Not my book. *Where did this come from?* I opened it, and written inside, in the upper right corner, as was his habit, was Neal's signature. Neal's book, then. On the next page was an inscription, "To Neal. Go with God."

Tears formed, of course. I didn't bother to name them.

There was no date or any other information to be seen. I didn't know the handwriting. The book was hefty, full of pictures. A coffee table book. No wonder I tripped over it. *How the hell did that book get in my hallway? And why? And when did my life become a damned Hitchcock film?*

Too bad I'm no cool blonde with a tiny waistline.

The electrician called to me.

The hallway was wrecked. I'd been so engrossed in the film noir of my life that I hadn't even heard the saws and hammers. A hole gaped toward the bottom of the wall.

"There's a nest of something in there chewing on your wires. Don't worry. I got Mrs. Denitch's permission. The wiring's fixed, but you need a trap. Someone else will have to come in to plaster the wall."

"Oh. Okay. So, the light's working?"

She pulled the chain and the bulb burned steadily. Not part of my ghost story then. I sighed and thanked her. "Is it mice?" I asked, as she packed up her tools.

"I'd say something bigger."

"But...there's a hole in my wall. Won't whatever it is come in my apartment?"

"I'll cover it for you. It'll be temporary, of course." Just then, she got a call. Obviously, someone needed her attention. She looked up apologetically. "The storm. It's made for a very busy morning. Could you...?" She indicated the hole.

"Cover it? Oh, yeah. No problem."

&

I swept up the mess. While I was looking for something to cover the hole, Mrs. Denitch dropped by to see the work and let me know that she'd already made calls to get the trap set and the hole repaired.

"Mrs. Denitch, I have a crazy question for you." I took a deep breath and said, "Has there ever been any evidence of this place being...haunted?"

Her blemished hands went to her cheeks, which had turned bright pink. Then she went pale.

I thought she might faint. "Are you okay?" I put an arm around her waist and led her into the living room. "I'm going to make you some tea."

Once we both had a steaming mug, I suggested we sit outside. The weather had turned balmy.

"Aly, I'm embarrassed, but also relieved by your question."

"Why?"

"Embarrassed because I rented out a haunted room! I just never thought anyone else would see him. He's never done anything bad as far as I know. I've seen him off and on for many, many years. Oh, not often. Perhaps ten times. I never told a soul. Of course, they wouldn't have believed me. That's where the relief comes in. Finally, someone else has seen him too. You have, haven't you?"

"Last night. During the thunderstorm."

"It's Holman, of course."

"You think?"

"Oh, I'm sure of it. I— Oh! Unless it was...could it have...you didn't think it was Neal, did you?" She whispered Neal's name.

It made me laugh. She looked at me quizzically.

"I've wondered before if he's tried to contact me, but I knew immediately that that man was not Neal...which is kind of neat, when you think of it."

"Why?"

"Because it means that even after death, we have an identifiable...self."

"That makes sense," she said seriously, and then we both burst into giggles. After agreeing that this was our little secret, she asked, "Will you stay even if the place is haunted?"

My Mews

"Yes, I will. I think I'm your perfect tenant."

☙

Later, I sat on the hall floor with a length of sturdy plastic and duct tape that Mrs. Denitch provided. I wiped down the wall with a damp rag and as I removed a piece of jagged plaster near the baseboard moulding, I saw something on the floor inside the wall. Thinking of large rodents with buck teeth, I recoiled.

It's flat, you ninny. Not an animal.

Gingerly, I reached in and grabbed a dusty book. I wiped it with my rag and realized that it wasn't a book after all, but a kind of portfolio, made of brown leather tooled with elaborate swirls and over-worked in delicate gold paint. The top was folded over and attached with a strap wound around a brass button. It looked like a man's possession.

Holman!

After peering in the hole to make sure there were no other treasures, I patched the opening as quickly as I could and was soon on the balcony ready to investigate.

The day, bright and mild, made my heart lighten for the first time in a long while. I almost allowed this unexpected joy to scare me, almost let myself slide oh-so-easily into the comfortable pit that I'd inhabited since Neal abruptly vanished. But I didn't. This time, I didn't.

I unwound the leather strip, lifted the flap and peeked inside. It was full of papers. Tilting the portfolio, I guided them out, onto the table. Letters, manuscripts, newspaper clippings. A tiny birth announcement trimmed in blue and gold. Beautiful, delicate keepsakes.

I picked up a letter and read,

My Dearest Holman,

My heart beats a syncopated rhythm in anticipation of your arrival. I have made a special treat for you. Sweets for the sweet. Does your love give you wings? For I feel

Nancy S.M. Waldman

*that I could fly. If only we could. Soon, my love, we will
be together. Forever.*

*With all the love I have to give, now and forever, I am
and remain*

Maggie, your future wife and the luckiest girl in the world

For all its flowery exuberance, the letter could have
been written by me to Neal during our courtship. I had recently
read our every email, every chat. The words would have been
different, but the excessive sticky-sweetness of new love had
not changed.

*So, Holman, the dashing horseman, was sentimental
enough to save his love letters. What else?*

I leafed through but didn't stop to read the other letters,
perhaps a dozen in all. The birth announcement, on a tiny
card not two inches in length read:

Eleanor
her happy arrival on
July 24, 1918
7 lbs 4 oz

Then, I came to the newspaper clippings and my heart
sank. Baby Eleanor, dead of the Spanish influenza, May 1919.
The revolt of the Bolsheviks. World War I news—bad and good.
The sinking of the Titanic. A devastating factory fire in New
York. Several articles on the world-wide influenza pandemic.
And then, with dread, I came to Maggie Stephens Taylor's
obituary. 1921. But not of the flu. She died from injuries after
being trampled by a horse. She was 20.

Oh, Holman, you poor soul.

Tears flowed, but for once, they weren't for me.

I gathered up the papers, carefully tucking them into
the leather pouch, and went inside. I walked slowly around my
apartment, talking to the stableman.

"We lost them too young. Are you still grieving all these
years later? Two deaths in such a short time. Your wife,
dying—oh, my God! It was one of your horses, wasn't it? How
could you stand it?"

I found myself opening cupboards and peering deeply
into the closets. Not running from my ghost, but wanting him,

needing to see him, to put my arms around him, a man who needed comfort so badly that his soul had never rested.

"So, the light, the light coming off and on, and—oh—you pointed that direction. You were trying to get me to uncover your little stash. But, the book? What is that about?"

The book was on my bedside table. I was almost halfway through it. The author talked about the soul as if it were just another part of us that needs tending to, like our skin or gall bladder. It talked about enoughness and saturation and solitude and austerity and abundance and all kinds of interesting ideas that took me out of my misery pit and put me some place new.

I opened it to the bookmark I'd left in it last night.

"How would you know about this book, Holman? I mean, you... what? Read all the books in the house and—"

An almost painful chill ran down my spine. I slammed the book shut and mashed it to my chest. My heart beat, beat, beat against the cover. Words, in the same rhythm, drummed in my mind. *Oh my God. Oh my God. Oh my God. It* was *Neal. It was Neal. Oh my God.*

I raised my face to the ceiling and looked around.

"Neal?"

Ridiculous, Aly. What? I expected Neal-with-wings to be hovering over me? What did I think was going to happen?

It already had happened.

Neal—through Holman—had given me a way to move forward. I had my sign. I had gotten the message and it had helped. It wasn't enough, but it was good. And, I didn't even cry.

The absence of tears because your dead husband communicated with you from the grave?

We'll just call that *acceptance.*

☙

☙ Grey Area ☙

Nancy S.M. Waldman

"Your place sparkles. You've been cleaning like a crazy woman," Sara said, picking up her drink from the kitchen and sitting down on the couch.

It had been a month since I'd found Holman's things. Sara knew all about the ways that my mental health had been improving, but not why. She thought it was "tincture of time" because I'd left out details such as a haunted apartment and messages from the dead.

"I have something you'll like," I said. I walked to the bedroom and came back holding my surprise.

"A puppy!" Sara squealed. "Oh my God. Cute!"

She took the tiny bundle of creamy brown mutt from my arms and ran to the balcony. The French doors were open and a sweet breeze wafted in.

How did I ever get so lucky to find this place?

The immediate remembrance of my absolute worst luck in the world—losing my husband at such a young age—came to me, but immediately drifted off. Lucky. Unlucky. Both true. Tonight, I made the choice to acknowledge the lucky me. I followed Sara outside.

"Is it a girl or boy? Have you named it?"

"Eleanor."

"What a funny, proper name for such a little cutie."

Sara was gone, head-over-heels in love with my dog.

Me too.

"It was either Tippy, Ingrid or that."

I ignored her questioning look and kept talking. "I have plans. I've decided to write. I mean really write. I have the freedom until the money runs out, right? By that time, maybe I'll have written and published at least one novel to great acclaim and fantastic future royalties."

"Yay!" Sara flung out an arm to hug me, but then went right back to lavishing attention on Eleanor. "What will you write?"

"Historical fiction. I have a plan, but I won't talk about it much. Might jinx it."

Holman and I had come to an understanding. He needed his story told and, miraculously, the universe had conspired to put me—a person who could tell a story and who could understand him and his misery—in this place.

His place. Our place.

That night after Sara left and I'd tucked Eleanor away in her kennel, I crawled into bed, tired and happy. The sheets smelled of sunshine from having hung on Mrs. Denitch's clothesline. I rolled onto my side so that I could look at the stars through the burgeoning oak leaves silhouetted against the street lights and, beyond all that, a clear sky.

I felt the presence behind me.

Used to it now, I settled back and drifted off, comforted and sure in my place, the place that I intended to stay. For now. For the rest of my life. Forever.

NANCY WALDMAN grew up in Texas, but has lived with her husband Barry in a 113 year-old "painted lady" house in the woods of Cape Breton for 12 years. She prefers the moderate cold of Nova Scotia over the extreme heat of Texas, but definitely misses Houston's ethnic restaurants and spreading oaks. Her short fiction has appeared in *The Speculative Elements* series by Third Person Press, *The Nashwaak Review*, *The Men's Breakfast*, and, soon, *Wild Violets Literary Magazine*. She is one of founders of Third Person Press, a member of The Quillians online writing and podcasting group and is a participant in the VP-XVII class of the Viable Paradise Writing Workshop on Martha's Vineyard. She's working on a SF novel about symbiotic aliens and brain plasticity. Visit her writing site at nancysmwaldman.com and on Twitter @nuanc.

A Glimpse of Light

Meggan Howatson

Being at a second-hand store helping my six-year-old sister pick out a Halloween costume was a task that most other guys my age would complain about. But Mom promised extra allowance that week if I went shopping and trick-or-treating with my sister, so I agreed, even if I did drag my heels about it. I liked Halloween, but I wasn't a kid anymore. This time around, I was in it for the money, though stocking up on candy wasn't such a bad thing either.

I looked over at my sister Shirley eyeing a rack of costumes, her smile increasing every time her gaze came to rest on a particular angel costume. I walked over and stood at her side for a moment. She was silent, her eyes fixed on the long white dress with lacy wings.

"Is that the one you want?"

"Yes." She looked up at me as if she were seeking my permission.

"Let's get it then."

A contagious smile blossomed on her face as she picked the costume up off the rack.

Meggan Howatson

As I paid—with Mom's money, of course—I listened to the conversation going on at the next register, turning my head slightly to hear better. My eyes wandered to the elderly cashier.

"That's right. The barrier between the living and the dead is at its weakest this time of year. Watch yourself, lad," the cashier said, handing a young boy his shopping bag. "And, have fun."

The words instantly brought me back to those stories Grandfather told. I used to sit in his dark living room, listening to his hypnotizing, raspy voice as he invented his tales. The great thing about Grandpa's stories was that they were always different. There were stories about animals, ghosts, great battles, and mythical creatures. Others were old Scottish legends and myths. He had a vivid imagination. His Scottish accent always caught my attention and kept me on the edge of my seat. No one could tell stories like Grandpa could, but I never thought for a minute, even when I was younger, that the stories were true.

The cashier's comment was very similar to a spooky thing my grandfather used to say about this time of the year. I used to nag him to tell me about it as soon as the leaves turned.

"Halloween is a time when our world and the Otherworld overlap, Liam. The wall between the two becomes thin. And sometimes, the dead like to play tricks on the living," Grandpa would say, a gleam in his eye.

I remember staring up at him, fascinated. Of course, I knew Grandpa had always enjoyed a good prank himself. One day I went to his house after school and found his back door wide open. Usually I had to ring the doorbell and he would let me in, but this day I felt my stomach flip when that wasn't the case. I walked in, shouting Grandpa's name when I saw no sign of him. Then, I noticed a note on the table.

If you want to find your grandpa, follow these ten clues.
Beware. Danger awaits you.

I was only twelve, but luckily—even though the handwriting on the note was messy—I recognized it as

⚘ Grey Area ⚘

Grandpa's writing or I probably would have called the police. I felt myself relax. *Good try, Grandpa.*

After following the intricate clues, I found myself in the woods behind Grandpa's place, and there he stood, smiling as I approached.

"Welcome to my Thinking Place," he said with a goofy little bow. "I decided that you're now old enough to appreciate it."

He'd built a bench out there in the middle of a circle of trees. How peaceful it was being surrounded by nothing but nature. We used to sit on that bench and stare up at the sky for hours with the breeze rustling the trees and the birds chirping around us. It became our favourite storytelling spot. When Grandpa passed away, I went there on my own to enjoy some peace and quiet.

Out of all my family members, I had taken Grandpa's death the hardest. We were close, so, naturally, his passing was difficult to handle, but because I was a kid Mom and Dad didn't tell me his time was soon coming. That made it hurt worse. I never had the chance to say that painful, yet important goodbye. The empty feeling and regret remained with me even now.

I whipped my head back around when I felt my sister tug on my jacket.

"Liam, take your receipt."

Right. I smiled at the cashier, and took the piece of paper, stuffing it into the bag with the costume.

"What were you doing in there?" Shirley asked as we crossed the parking lot to get to the car. I sighed, and looked down at her, smiling at her curious expression.

"Listening, and just thinking of Grandpa."

I awoke with a start that night. A strange green light bobbled in mid-air. *Did it wake me up?* I rubbed my eyes to get the

Meggan Howatson

sleep out and glanced at the clock. *3:15 a.m.* It always freaked me out to wake up at that time. A lot of horror movies involved characters waking up at 3:15 and bad things always followed. I knew it was stupid to believe that time was cursed, but it's hard to remember that at 3:15 a.m.

I looked around. No green light. *Had I only dreamed it?*

I grabbed my flashlight, turned it on, and shone it around the room. Everything looked normal. My clothes were still in a messy pile in the corner. My posters were still motionless on the walls. I sighed and ran a hand through my bed-hair, and lay back down. I stared at the ceiling, then back at the clock. *3:17.* Whatever had been in my room—or maybe just in my head—would have cleared out by now if it was the typical horror movie creature.

I sighed again and mentally mocked myself. I was eighteen years old, for crying out loud. I should know by now that spirits and ghosts and monsters aren't real. Even though it was hard to ignore the sickening feeling in my stomach, I closed my eyes. *Go back to sleep, Liam. It was just a stupid dream.*

۞

I walked with Shirley, a bounce still in my sister's step as we approached the twenty-sixth house on the street. My costume consisted of a simple plaid shirt and my regular jeans.

"Liam, you're supposed to dress up." Mom had said before we left the house.

"I am. I'm a lumberjack."

She was unimpressed. I don't know why it's so hard for moms to realize that boys like me aren't children anymore.

Shirley let go of my hand and left me standing on the sidewalk as she trotted up the steps to our neighbour's house. She rang the doorbell.

"Trick or treat!" she yelled when Mrs. Edgerly opened the door to greet her.

"Oh, hello, there. What a beautiful little angel you make, Shirley. Let's just see what I can dig up for you." She stepped

۞ Grey Area ۞

A Glimpse of Light

back inside the house and Shirley waited patiently on the doorstep, her treat-filled pillowcase in hand.

I glanced up at the sky. It was fully dark. The sun hadn't even begun to set when we had left the house.

I felt a tug inside, a sudden longing for Grandpa. Maybe his stories were still swirling around in my subconscious. Or maybe I was just lonely for him because he had sometimes taken me out trick-or-treating when I was a kid.

I let out a sigh, and brought my gaze back down. My stomach turned and I felt a sudden flicker of suspicion when a small, familiar, green light glowed in front of my eyes. It went dim for a second and then shone brilliantly again as it flew toward the forest at the back of Mrs. Edgerly's house.

My arms suddenly felt cold and shaky. I watched the light and waited for it to disappear, as it had in my room that night, but my heart pounded when instead, it flew around in a circle—like a fairy might—and headed into the forest.

"Hey, hurry up. We need to go!" I called to Shirley as I jogged toward the doorstep.

"Why? I didn't get my treats yet. And I want to walk through the graveyard display!" Shirley whined, pointing to the plastic tombstones and goblins that Mrs. Edgerly had set up on her lawn.

"Come on. This is important." I took her small hand in my own. I could feel her questioning gaze on me, but ignored it. I sprinted down the steps, and headed into the forest, trying desperately to follow that tiny spark.

"Why so fast? Where are we going?" Shirley cried.

"I'll tell you later. Come on!" I scooped her onto my back and ran toward the dot of light. If it had been a movie, I would have been yelling at the character to run away because he or she would probably end up getting hurt or lost, or worse. But this was no movie and I was filled with confidence. That light was real, and I wouldn't be able to rest until I found out what it was.

Anyway, what's Halloween without a little haunting?

🍂 Grey Area 🍂

Meggan Howatson

I passed through the trees, catching a glimpse of that light every now and then. Finally, we made it to a clearing. We were on a circular piece of land, in plain view of the water.

"What is it?"

"See that light?" I whispered, pointing to the now dim circle that was hovering in the air, just metres away from my face.

"No," Shirley answered, sounding spooked.

"Sshhh...quiet. It's okay."

I stood very still and watched the light in amazement as it slowly took the shape of the old man I loved and admired. I could only see him from the back, but I knew it was him as he walked—or perhaps floated—out over the water. He turned his head to look at me, and he smiled. That bright gleam in his eye made me smile. I knew he was here, here to play one last trick on me. I raised a hand, and gave a slow wave, despite Shirley staring at me like I was crazy. Maybe I was.

"What is it?" my sister asked again. I said nothing, the smile never leaving my face. *It was Grandpa. Saying goodbye.* I gave a satisfied chuckle. I felt complete.

&

Shirley never said a word as we made our way out of the woods. I knew she was mad at me for pulling her away from Mrs. Edgerly's house, and I knew I'd scared her with my ghost chase.

I took her hand in mine and glanced down with a smile. "Sorry about that, Shirl. I just had to check something out."

She didn't look at me. Instead, she stared ahead, and her eyes grew wide. I followed her gaze.

Mrs. Edgerly's graveyard display was in ruin. Pieces of goblins were scattered across the grass. Several of the tombstones stood askew. In the middle of it all rested a car, its front bumper battered and smashed, its windshield shattered. Thick smoke rose from the vehicle, mixing with the cool night

& Grey Area &

A Glimpse of Light

air. Inside, the driver wasn't moving; his head rested lifelessly on the steering wheel.

I felt Shirley squeeze my hand. We were both silent for a long moment as we gazed upon the devastation. In the distance, we heard sirens. I turned my attention to the house. Through the window, I saw Mrs. Edgerly on the phone, looking frantic.

"That light..." Shirley peeped, "did it cause this?"

My mouth was dry as I spoke. "No." My mind wandered back to Grandpa and everything fell into place. "It saved us."

MEGGAN HOWATSON is a creative young writer from Sydney Mines who enjoys anything artsy. She recently completed her Bachelor of Arts degree at Cape Breton University, and is looking forward to attending a digital arts program in the fall. When she's not writing, she can be found playing videogames or increasing her musical repertoire. She likes horseback riding and hanging out with her closest friends. This is Meggan's first published story, and she looks forward to writing more stories in the future.

Night Swimmer

Leah Noble

All is still.

I hear my own breathing, and can feel that I'm lying down, curled up.

I move my neck, my hands, and begin to get up. But I'm struck with a headache—*am I hungover?* I can't remember a reason why I would be, because last night was a Wednesday and I would have been staying in. But, here I am, with a pounding pain all through my skull, a tight neck and no desire to get up.

Some time passes. I move my cheek against my pillow and realize it is not a pillow—it is grass. Soft, long grass, as in a field in August. I sit up with difficulty, my head complaining. I lean back against the headboard of my bed, but it is made of stone. I don't care to compute this. I'm too groggy, so I lean there for a little while.

My eyes are still closed when I hear a voice.

"Hi there," says a man. *This must be a very lucid dream,* I think, so I'm past caring what consequence my actions might have. I grunt at him like I would at my boyfriend if he woke me too early. Guttural and curt.

Leah Noble

"You must be in some pain."

I fight against feeling both hungover and drunk, trying to push away this fog in my head long enough to focus. I take a deep breath and open my eyes.

A man sits on a gravestone to my right. He's eating an apple, and the sound of his chewing irritates me. So sensual and crunchy. He's got a paperback held open with his thumb, and he's swinging one leg. La dee da, buddy.

"Who are you?"

"I'm your neighbour, you could say." He grins, showing pieces of apple between his teeth.

"Excuse me," I say, finding my politeness, "am I dreaming?"

He laughs. "You would be surprised how often I hear that."

I reach up and rub my temples. "You wouldn't happen to have any water, would you? I'm really thirsty."

He gets off his seat and goes a short distance away, then comes back with a glass filled with water, which I drink down in one mouthful. I feel it running down into my stomach, feel the coolness of it. It tastes sweet, like fresh maple sap.

I sit, just breathing, and looking out over a valley. On the opposite side is a highway, from here quite small. Ant-sized cars and trucks pass, reflecting the afternoon sun. My neighbour eats his apple and reads.

My headache subsides, and I can look around without my head hurting now. More gravestones in rows and a stand of apple trees rich with red fruit sit to the left. A young female deer grazes among the trees, her eyes intent on the ground.

Then it is night. I don't know how fast it turns, just that it has. I breathe in the scent of the late summer night, all ripe with hay and flowers and vegetable gardens. Faint noises, as if from people in their homes, reach my ears. Oddly, it isn't lonely, sitting there in the dark, with a stranger at the gravestone beside me. I look up and the sky is frothy with stars. A few shoot across in split seconds

My neighbour speaks. "Okay, Helena, it's time for us to talk."

🐌 *Grey Area* 🐌

Night Swimmer

He knows my name, and I feel somewhat sad, like he is an old friend I've lost touch with. He hands me a blanket, which I wrap around my shoulders.

"You're here because you've passed over."

I nod. *Why doesn't this surprise me?*

"Do you have any memory of that happening?"

I don't at first. Then something comes to me.

Driving my car.

I had come to enjoy the solitude of the long drives home from work. I had moved out to the West Mountains, to be with my boyfriend, Paul. It was an hour's drive from his cabin in the woods to the city where I worked. While I hated knowing what my driving was doing to the atmosphere, I did love my little black Ford, how she took me over the bridges and out of the city, through traffic and along the highway, then up the dirt road to Paul's cabin. Sometimes I'd sit for a few seconds after I'd turned the engine off, and hear the tickings of the car settling in.

Then I would jump from the car, gather my things and climb the stairs to the deck. Paul had built his home within a stand of tall birch trees, on the edge of a spruce forest, so that the deck was up in the trees. In summer, with all the leaves out, it was covered in a green canopy, and dappled in shade. Our dog Becca would run out the screen door, greeting me with her golden retriever love. And Paul would be in the kitchen, carefully slicing something—a long, white leek or a rich orange carrot.

"Hey babe," he would call, and I would take off my shoes and go to him, wrapping my arms around him from behind, resting my head on his shoulders, kissing his neck. I would breathe in, soaking up his strength, his solidness, his smell.

He would pretend to be cranky—saying "I'm cooking here!" in a fake Italian accent—and I would laugh and tell him about my day while I picked at his tidy piles of chopped vegetables. Then I'd rub Becca's head and tell her what a good dog, what a beautiful dog, she was. Sooner or later I would turn on my laptop and check blogs and sites, getting lost in the

Leah Noble

lovely pictures of other people's lives, clicking through and not wanting to look away. Before I knew it an hour would have gone by, and it would be time for supper. The golden light on the deck would have shifted.

"I was driving, and a transport truck came up too fast. The last thing I remember is its grille growing too large in my rearview mirror." I say this in the dark, to my neighbour.

"There was a crash," he says.

"Was it my fault?"

"Do you need to know?"

I realize that I don't. It doesn't matter.

"Where is Paul?" I feel sick all of a sudden. An ache rises up, a long lonesomeness. The urge to cry comes on like a summer thunderstorm.

"Paul is where you found him, in his house in the trees. And he misses you, but he's doing okay."

I'm not sure which I want less to be true, that he's sad without me, or that he's moving on. I push up from the ground and walk away.

"Helena, you can walk away, but you can't get away." Then, silence.

I wrap the blanket around me and walk through the field. On the horizon is light; it will be dawn soon. I turn and look behind me, and can see the West Mountains in the distance. A few lights sprinkle over them, and the city glows even farther beyond. I realize that I am in the county where I grew up, East River County. I haven't been here in years. I walk down into the valley, towards the flat, cool river I know is there.

On my way through the field, my toes fill with bug spit, and I disturb the last of the night's fireflies, which glow green down in the grass. The field comes to a road, and I cross. Early workers' cars pass, and no-one looks at me, no-one bats an eyelash at a strange girl wrapped in a blanket walking barefoot through the fields, at dawn. Yet the texture of the asphalt under my feet feels real.

Once off the hill, I walk through a mature forest, tall oaks with wide trunks. I am close to the river because I can

Night Swimmer

hear it rushing over rocks in its thin parts. I walk farther and push through a dense bank of alders, and then I am at the river's edge. Here is a pool, and the banks are smooth from people's steps. A rope hangs straight down from a tree limb. The river continues to flow through this spot, even though it is just daybreak and there are no parties of rambunctious children to splash into it.

Sitting down on a flat stone by the edge, I rub my eyes the way I always have for relief and rest. I think, *the way I did when I was alive*, and this all suddenly feels surreal. I dip my toes in the river, feel the cool water on them. At least that is still true.

"Helena."

I turn around, thinking it will be my strange neighbour, but it is Paul. He is walking toward me wearing pyjamas. His feet are bare.

I get to my feet quickly and run to him. He hugs me and I hold him tight. He feels as he has always felt. Strong. Solid. I tuck my nose into his neck and breathe him in. His special smell, the warmth of his skin.

He runs a hand through my hair and I think my heart might actually crack through like the trunk of a tree.

"Am I dreaming?" he asks me. "I must be."

"I don't know." Then I start laughing. Giddiness rushes up and swallows me. "I think this is just a big weird dream! And we're going to wake up soon, and Becca will be in bed, like, farting, and that's why we're having this weird dream!"

We both start laughing and then I look and he's crying.

"No, dear. No," he says.

I realize I'm breathing in jags, trying to spit out the laughter, trying to reset my emotions.

"I think *I'm* dreaming," he continues. "I fell asleep on the couch tonight even though Becca wouldn't stop barking at the door. I opened it and saw a man holding a book and an apple. He got me into his car. And I was all like, "Hey, I'm sleepin' here!"

I giggle, to relieve my tension.

⊱ Grey Area ⊰

Leah Noble

"But he said I had to come. Only it was your car, and that's when I knew I was dreaming, because your car was totalled."

I don't say anything, just look at him and listen. I feel deep and still, like the river.

"We drove and drove. Well, I drove and he read his book, and told me when to turn. We drove out to your parents' old place, and then past it, onto this dirt road. And he said where to park and to walk along this path. So I did and here I am."

We stand there for a long time, and the sun comes up. The morning mists rise around us and disperse, and the birds begin their day in earnest, spattering the air with tweets and twitters. We walk along the river, we throw in rocks. Sometimes we talk, sometimes we kiss. We make love under a tree, where there is soft moss to lie on. Like always, we forget everything else when we are naked together, physically working towards a common, sweet goal.

It is afternoon when my neighbour finds us napping together.

He taps me on the shoulder. "Helena, it's time to go."

"I am not ready," I say, hoping that this is how it works: if you aren't ready they don't take you.

"If that's how it worked, none of us would ever go."

I look beside me where Paul was sleeping, but he is no longer there. I know he is on the old couch, with the sun just setting through the window. I see the plants on the windowsill, the colors of the art on the wall. I see Becca relaxed and asleep in front of the door, still guarding. I see Paul's face asleep, his eyes and eyelids and the bones of his cheeks. How handsome he is.

My neighbour walks beside me while we go to the river. The sun has set and we are now in semi-dusk.

"So this is how it's done?" I say. I am less sad now because I'm grateful that I get to see this miracle. Everyone still alive has no idea, but I will.

🍃 Grey Area 🍃

Night Swimmer

"Well, this is how it's done for you." He says. "No-one's death is the same. Except for the very last part, which will happen when you close your eyes."

I walk into the river. It's cool and soothing, as if I had a sunburn. I sink into it up to my shoulders, and dip my face in. Then I lie backwards. This was always my favorite thing to do, when swimming: floating on my back, looking up at the sky and hearing only water, the rest of the world quiet. Feeling supported, and moved slightly by the current.

As my eyes close, I feel myself disintegrating and becoming water. My hands, my arms, my breasts and my belly are all water. My love for Paul, for the mountains, for my living self, all of these join the river and flow away.

LEAH NOBLE grew up in Baddeck, NS, and now makes her home in North Sydney. She is a Graphic Design student at the Nova Scotia Community College in Sydney. She has worked as a waitress, a nanny, a potter's assistant and a store manager at a marina. Her blog is "Dream Big Cape Breton" (www.dreambigcapebreton.com) and this is her first short story in print.

ePrayer

Sherry D. Ramsey

"Hello?"

Larry jumped as the voice sounded in his headset, his index finger reflexively clicking the mouse button and accidentally closing the document he had open. *Damn.* He hadn't even realized the line was ringing. He glanced at the opening of his cubicle, but fortunately no-one was watching him.

Recovering, he launched into the answering protocol. "Hello, and thank you for calling ePrayer, where we care about your Life...and your Afterlife. My name is Larry. How can I help you today?"

Silence. Then, "ePrayer?" the voice asked hesitantly.

"That's right," Larry said smoothly, re-opening the file showing the day's preset patter. "The world's largest provider of spoken electronic prayer services. You picked an auspicious day to call ePrayer, sir, because today we're offering new customers a special package. Any two prayers from your chosen religion or belief system, plus a new prayer for world peace, for one low monthly rate. They'll be offered up daily in your name by our dedicated servers—"

"I'm...I'm already a customer," the man's voice said.

Sherry D. Ramsey

"Wonderful," Larry said, quickly switching mental gears—and patter. "Then you might be interested in our new buy-one-month, get-one-month free offer. It applies to any prayer of your choice, any religion, and it will be repeated as many times as you specify, daily for the full two-month period. This is really an unbeatable—"

"Did you say your name was Larry?"

"Yes, sir, and I'm here to—"

"Larry, could you just be quiet for a minute?"

Larry took a breath and bit his lip. That was...unusual. He pursed his lips and clicked to the "Dissatisfied Customers" protocol. A glance down the list didn't reveal anything helpful. The voice wasn't angry, crying, or offended, hadn't demanded anything, wasn't asking to speak to his supervisor, didn't seem to be a crank.

"Uh, sure," he said quietly.

After a moment's silence, the voice said, "Okay, Larry, can you look up my file for me?"

Well, that was something he could handle. "No problem, sir. Your name?"

"Henry Rutherford."

Larry's fingers skittered across the keyboard as he input the data. "I show five Henry Rutherfords on file, sir. Middle initial?"

"V."

"Thank you, sir. Code word?"

The voice hesitated again. "Phoenix."

"Thank you. Okay, I have your file open, Mr. Rutherford. What can I do to help you?" Now maybe this weird call would get on track.

"Can you tell me what prayers I've paid for in the past, Larry?" When Larry didn't answer right away, the voice chuckled. "Old men have short memories sometimes."

"Uh, sure. Our servers recited six months of 'Prayers for Departed Loved Ones' on your behalf just over two years ago, and we've been doing 'Supplications to Cure Illness' for the past year. And I show a non-standard special prayer that you must have written yourself, which we've been incanting twice daily for two months now."

"That would be the *I-don't-want-to-die* prayer," Mr. Rutherford said.

"Uh...if you say so, Mr. Rutherford. I don't have the specifics here in this file." Larry glanced at the cubicle "doorway" again, this time wishing one of the supervisors *would* be there.

"Well, I guess it worked—sort of."

The incoming call signal beeped in Larry's headset and his red line light lit up. He frowned at it. There was no way he should be getting another call when he was already dealing with a client. He decided to ignore it.

"You'd better get that, Larry," Mr. Rutherford said. "I can wait."

Huh? There was also no way the client would be able to hear the signal from another call. Then Larry noticed that no line glowed red for Mr. Rutherford's call. Double weird. Hoping for the best, Larry pressed the "hold" button and took the new call.

He made it only halfway through the answering protocol when a woman's voice interrupted, said she had a wrong number, and hung up abruptly. He sighed and looked down at his phone, wondering how to go back to Mr. Rutherford since none of the lines seemed to be active. He hoped he hadn't cut the old guy off. That would look bad.

"Everything okay, Lawrence?"

Larry's supervisor, Andrea, had a soft voice and an even softer step. He whirled in his chair, feeling his face prickle with heat. He hadn't heard her outside his cubicle.

The last thing Larry wanted was to look bad in front of Andrea, who had dark brown hair, eyes to match, and a smile that haunted his dreams. He forced a rueful smile and tried to banish his blush by pure force of will.

"Sure, just a wrong number. They didn't even give me a chance to finish my intro!"

Sherry D. Ramsey

Andrea returned his smile with her own, the one that always made his heart secretly melt in his chest. "Better luck next time!"

While Larry mentally dithered, wondering if this would be a good time to ask her out for coffee, she gave him a little wave and moved on down the row of cubicles. He closed his eyes and sagged in his chair. Too late off the mark again.

ePrayer had no restrictions about employees dating— Larry had checked. The only restriction he seemed to keep running into was the one that kept his brain from engaging his mouth like a normal human when Andrea was around.

He suddenly remembered Henry and frowned at his phone. Experimentally, he pressed the "hold" button again.

"I'm still here, Larry."

"Oh, great!" Larry leaned back in his chair. "So did you want to renew your subscription, sir, or can I start a new prayer cycle for you?"

"Hmmm. Neither, Larry. I don't think I'll be needing any more prayers at all."

"We'd hate to lose you as a customer, sir. Is there anything—"

Mr. Rutherford cut him off again, just like the wrong number lady. The old guy had an annoying habit of doing that. "Oh, you won't be losing me, Larry," he said with the ghost of a chuckle. "I think I'll let you go now, but I'll call again. Thanks for your help. Have a good day."

There was no click or signal that the connection had been broken, but Larry felt a strange certainty that Mr. Rutherford had left the conversation. He heaved a deep sigh. Hopefully that one hadn't been recorded for quality control. He had no idea if he'd handled it correctly or not. With luck, the man would get a different associate if he did call back.

☞

When Larry arrived at work the next morning, he had to detour from his usual route through the ePrayer building because

☞ Grey Area ☞

they were still waxing some of the floors. It meant he had to pass the server rooms, which he usually tried to avoid. As soon as he entered the hallway, the stilted muttering of text-to-speech electronic voices filled the air. He always wished they could soundproof the rooms, but of course that wouldn't make much sense—the point of the voices was to be heard, right? *Then again, couldn't God hear through a soundproofed wall?* Eventually he'd stopped thinking about it because it made his head hurt. Usually he just took the long way around to the elevators.

Today, though, he couldn't avoid the voices. The din really didn't sound terribly devotional. Cacophonous was more like it, with hundreds of computers intoning different prayers, in different languages, at the same time. ePrayer tried hard to walk the line between catering to the requirements of each religion and being inclusive; they didn't keep separate rooms for different faith denomination servers. Part of that was practical use of space. They did, however, observe niceties like geographical orientations and the use of various prayer paraphernalia for faith-dedicated servers. Some of the servers bore holographic stickers of stylized religious symbols, which flashed in the overhead lights as Larry passed.

The voices battered against Larry's ears as he passed the rooms. Clients had many options to make sure their prayers were intoned just as they'd like: male or female voices, over sixty languages, hundreds of accents and dialects. Only a word here and there rang clearly over the devotional tumult.

"—peace to all—"

"—grant us humility—"

"—ease our suffering—"

"—multitude of blessings—"

The server room was separated from the hallway by a long wall that was mostly windows. An ePrayer employee in a cleansuit moved among the racks of machines, collecting last night's backup discs for shipping offsite and loading up the new ones. Larry couldn't imagine how loud the noise must be right inside the room. Miniature multicolored prayer flags fluttered here and there in the breeze from the cooling system.

Sherry D. Ramsey

He suppressed an urge to run to get out of earshot and steeled himself to a normal, measured pace. Somehow, the voices always sounded reproachful. Maybe because even though he worked here, he had his doubts about the efficacy of computer-generated prayers. He shook himself. *What's wrong with me?* They were computers, inanimate objects, simply doing what they were programmed to do. They had no idea of his existence, let alone that he was passing through the hallway.

Still, he pulled in a deep breath and huffed it out in relief when he settled into his desk chair and slid on his headset.

"Good morning, Larry," said Henry Rutherford's voice in his ears before Larry's workstation had even finished booting up.

Larry almost jumped up from his chair, but managed to limit himself to grabbing the armrests for support. He didn't want to attract any attention by having his head suddenly pop up above his cubicle walls. "Mr. Rutherford?" he answered, just above a whisper.

A low chuckle. "Yep, it's me. I've been waiting for you to come in."

Larry's phone console lay dark, no red lights blinking. "Where are you, sir?" he asked slowly. None of this made sense. "My computer's not even fully on yet."

"That's actually a very good question, Larry, and one I'm not sure I can answer myself. I seem to be in your system."

Larry frowned. "You're tapped into the ePrayer system? You mean, like, the phone lines are crossed or something?"

"Not exactly."

"You—you hacked us? That shouldn't be possible. We're a closed internal network." Why would anyone hack an electronic prayer service anyway? Unless he was some kind of nut, but Mr. Rutherford didn't sound unbalanced.

He did sound slightly exasperated. "I wouldn't know how to hack a peanut butter sandwich, son. I mean actually *in* the system. Larry, could you open up my file again?"

ePrayer

The computer had finished its boot cycle and sat waiting for him to enter something. Still bemused, he called up the file in question. "Okay, I have it."

"Would you check the billing information for me, Larry?"

"Sure." Larry clicked to the billing screen and his frown deepened. "This is weird."

"What does it say?"

"There's a termination notice set for about a month's time..."

"Anything else?"

Larry swallowed. "Until then there's just one active request—another round of 'Prayers for Departed Loved Ones,' but—"

"They're for me this time, aren't they, Larry? It's okay. I had pretty much figured out that I must be dead."

Larry tore off the headset and dropped it on the desk as if it were a snake.

"Lawrence? Something wrong?"

Andrea again. Her face showed concern, her clear brown eyes puzzled as she glanced at the headset on the desk.

Yeah, there's a ghost in the system. But he couldn't say that. He didn't even believe it, not really. Sweat prickled his forehead and he felt his face begin another slow burn as he picked up his headset and tried to cover it with a chuckle. "Sure. Fine," he said. "Got some kind of...some kind of shock from the headset, that's all." He frowned at it and pretended to examine the wires.

Andrea frowned. "That's strange. Better requisition a replacement," she said. "Has that happened before?"

"No." He shook his head. "I'll see if this one will last the shift, anyway." Mentally he kicked himself. She was never going to go out with him if he impressed her as a troublemaker.

"Okay, let me know if it keeps acting up," she told him. "Have a good day."

"You too," he said, trying to look distracted by the headset. As soon as she disappeared around the corner he carefully put the headset down on his desk and stared at it.

🫖 Grey Area 🫖

Sherry D. Ramsey

The red linelight flashed on and he almost jumped again. Larry closed his eyes and shook his head. *Get hold of yourself, man. You're imagining stuff. Or this is some kind of prank. No such thing as ghosts. If you don't take calls you're going to get fired, or at least get Andrea mad at you.*

He forced himself to reach out and pick up the headset again, although his hand trembled a bit. He slipped it on, and blew out a sigh of relief when it stayed silent. Henry—or whoever it was—seemed to be gone again. He closed Henry Rutherford's file, pulled up the days' script, and punched the button to take the call. He also surreptitiously glanced around his cubicle, trying to spot a hidden camera. Was a video of him tearing off the headset going to show up on YouTube?

"Hello, and thank you for calling ePrayer, where we care about your Life...and your Afterlife. My name is Larry. How can I help you today?"

Don't be Henry, don't be Henry, don't be Henry—

It wasn't Henry. It was a lovely, polite elderly lady who wanted to set up an account to say prayers for her while she had surgery. The normalcy of the whole thing felt wonderful, and Larry felt the knots in his stomach relaxing as he set up her file, took her credit card information, and put her on the email list for special prayer offers. By the time the call ended, the tension between his shoulder blades had almost completely disappeared.

Larry slid the headphones off so they hung around his neck, and rubbed a hand across his face. The whole Henry thing had to be some kind of elaborate prank. The problem was, he didn't know anyone who seemed at all likely to do such a thing.

I'm sorry. The letters sprang up on his screen, in the notepad window he always kept running in the sidebar for quick notes. *I truly did not mean to upset you, Larry. But I do think I need some help, and I trust you. Let me know when we can talk again. Henry R.*

Somehow the note was much less unnerving than the voice in his headphones, even though there was no way it should be just writing itself when no-one was even touching

ePrayer

his keyboard. He wondered fleetingly if it could still be the result of a prank, but in his heart he knew it wasn't.

He closed the notepad so anyone walking past wouldn't see it, took the headphones off altogether and put his phone into "AFK" mode. He had ten minutes to get back to his desk before the break expired. His first stop was the bathroom, where he splashed cool water on his face and stared in the mirror for thirty seconds. He didn't look crazy. Then he visited the break room, poured up a travel mug full of hot coffee and added cream and sugar, just the way he liked it. By the time he got back to his desk and took a sip of coffee, he felt better. He slid the headphones on and reactivated his phone, but until his line lit up, he was free.

He restored the notepad and looked at the message for a moment, then took a deep breath and typed, *What kind of help do you need, Henry?*

The delay in the answer wasn't more than five seconds. *I seem to be stuck in the ePrayer servers, and I want to get out of here.*

Fair enough. *But you are dead, right, Henry? You are—whatever is left of Henry V. Rutherford, some part that has somehow survived death. A...ghost?*

I wouldn't like to say that for sure, Henry answered, *but I'm sure not in Kansas anymore. :)*

Larry actually caught himself chuckling. The old guy had a sense of humour, anyway. Apparently God did, too. The old guy hadn't wanted to die, so he was still around...sort of.

Any idea how I could get you out?

Seems to be a closed system in here. No network or Internet access. I've been all through it.

Larry nodded, then remembered that Henry couldn't see him. Or, at least, he figured Henry couldn't see him. He hoped not. That would make things all the more creepy and unbelievable.

Security, Larry said. *The prayer servers are a closed loop. No chance someone who doesn't like us can hack in and mess up people's prayers.*

I wonder if I'd fit on a USB stick?

⬈ Grey Area ⬈

Larry laughed out loud, then quickly put a hand over his mouth and looked around guiltily. He hoped no-one—especially Andrea—had heard that and thought he was laughing at a client.

The red line light pulsed to life.

I have to take a call, Henry, Larry typed, *but tomorrow I'll bring one and we'll see what happens, okay?*

Appreciate it, Larry. Talk later. And Henry was gone again.

It wasn't until he got home that night that Larry remembered he wasn't permitted to bring a USB stick to work, as part of the security protocols for protecting the ePrayer system. However, security was actually pretty lax—it wasn't like anyone ever searched pockets or bags. He shrugged. It would be a minor breach, and he figured he could do it without getting caught. Now that he believed Henry's story, he couldn't bring himself to leave the old guy stuck in the system without at least trying to help him.

He tucked the stick into his lunch bag in preparation for the next morning. Hopefully four gigabytes of space would be enough.

Despite his efforts to convince himself that taking the USB stick in to work was no big deal, Larry found himself sweating uncomfortably as he entered the ePrayer building the next morning. Chuck, the security guard, looked up and greeted Larry with his customary nod and grunt. Larry thought Chuck's eyes lingered on the lunch bag, but of course that was silly. It was the same lunch bag he brought to work every single day. There was no reason for Chuck to take any special notice of it today.

Larry sighed inwardly when Chuck turned his gaze back to his magazine without another word. *Past the first checkpoint.* He reached his cubicle without further incident and sank into his chair, setting the lunch bag on the floor near his feet. All he had to do was watch for his chance, sneak Henry onto the USB, and get out safely at the end of the day. No big deal.

He hoped. As his computer finished its startup routine and he slipped on the headphones, a note popped up on his screen. *Larry?*

All set, Larry answered hurriedly. *Just going to watch for a good opportunity.*

I'll be here. The window disappeared again. The line light went red, and Larry answered his first call of the day.

The perfect opportunity to try to rescue Henry came at break time. It was Saria's birthday, apparently, and someone had brought a cake. No-one in his unit would notice his absence, though. When he heard them start to sing at her cubicle on the other side of the room, he glanced around to make sure he was alone, and slipped the USB stick out of his bag. He had to unplug his mouse to open a port for it, so he opened the note window first.

Henry, you there? I'm plugging in now, he typed.

I see it, came the reply.

A blue light blinked on the stick, indicating that it was active, but it went on so long that Larry felt sweat trickle along his spine. The singing had stopped and now all he heard was general chatter as people shared out cake and made jokes about getting older.

"Not at the party, Lawrence?" came a voice from his cubicle opening.

Andrea. He managed not to jump, and twirled his chair so that his body might block the blinking USB stick. "I'm trying to eat a little healthier," he said with what he hoped was a charming smile, and patted his stomach. At least she couldn't see how it roiled in fear of being discovered. "No cake for you, either?"

She smiled and held up an icing-stained napkin. "I had a half piece. The store-bought variety is a little too sweet for me. But it's bad luck not to eat birthday cake, you know."

Wish I'd known that earlier, Larry thought. He had to get rid of her before she noticed the blinking blue light. "I'll remember that next time," he said lamely.

❧ *Grey Area* ❧

Sherry D. Ramsey

"Headset working okay now?" she asked, leaning lightly against one of the precarious cubicle walls.

"Oh! Yeah, fine," he said. *Why would she pick right now to hang around?* He prayed that Henry didn't start messaging him on the screen. There was no way she'd miss that.

Andrea glanced down the cubicle hallway, then back at Larry. She looked down at her napkin quickly again, chewing her lower lip. She wanted to say something, Larry could see, but what? She was pretty straightforward when it came to work issues. Was it really that big a deal that he hadn't joined the others for cake?

She obviously came to some kind of decision, because she looked back up, smiled, and said, "Well, see you later," then walked off quickly.

Larry slumped in his chair, the perspiration on his back suddenly cold. He shivered. He swung around and saw that the blue light had gone dark.

Henry?

They hadn't made a plan for how Henry would communicate with him if he'd made it onto the USB stick. He slipped on the headset and said "Henry?" in a low voice.

"*File too large,*" came Henry's voice, punctuated with a sigh. "I couldn't fit. It was like trying to pour a bottle of vodka into a shot glass. Guess we need another idea, Larry."

Dammit. "I'll try another one tomorrow, Henry. One with more space. Are you going to be okay until then?"

"I'll be fine," Henry said. "In fact, I discovered something rather interesting last night."

"Something in the system?"

"Lawrence? Who are you talking to?" Andrea's voice sounded behind him, puzzled and suspicious.

Double dammit. He hadn't heard her come back. He spun his chair slowly to face her, slipping the headset off and hoping she hadn't noticed the USB, which still stuck out of his mouse port. Her face seemed colder as she looked at him. Personal calls were strictly forbidden on the incoming lines. There were phones in the locker room for employees to use, and almost everyone had a cell phone these days, anyway, although they were supposed to leave the building to use them so as not to risk any interference with the prayers.

"It's...er, sorry," he stammered. "I...um, my uncle called...he's kind of senile. He didn't realize it wasn't allowed. I was just getting him off the line." He smiled weakly at her.

The wrinkles of concern in her forehead didn't smooth. If anything, she looked more suspicious. "He called you? What are the chances he'd actually get *you* to answer instead of someone else?"

Larry forced a weak chuckle. "Heh, I know. Crazy coincidence, huh?" *Please don't notice the USB stick.* If she saw that, there was no way he could talk himself out of trouble.

She put her hands on her hips, her look changing to sorrowful. "You know we have a zero tolerance policy, Lawrence," she said. "I have to report this."

"I know you *should*," Larry agreed. "But it was only a few seconds, honestly. I mean, you know that, you were just here and I wasn't on the phone then."

She pursed her lips and looked down. She still held the balled-up napkin from her piece of cake. "That's true," she admitted.

"I'll make sure it doesn't happen again." He hated the pleading note in his voice, but he couldn't help it. He didn't think he'd get fired for one little infraction of the rules, but he didn't want a black mark or warning on his record.

"Okay, just this once," she said with a sigh. "I can't do anything if it happens again."

"Thanks," he said, relief flooding him. He smiled at her with genuine appreciation. "I really appreciate this."

She didn't return the smile, just nodded once and turned away from the cubicle. As soon as she was gone, Larry yanked the USB stick out of the port without bothering to properly eject it, and stuffed it into his pocket. He plugged his mouse back in and collapsed back into his chair, running a hand over his face. *That was close.*

It wasn't until then that he wondered what Andrea had come back to say.

⚘ Grey Area ⚘

A message popped up on his notepad window. *Sorry. I heard all that through the headset.*

Don't worry about it, Larry typed. *We'll figure something out.*

He just wasn't sure what. And he hoped it wasn't going to cost him his job.

🦀

Larry shook off a feeling of dread as he slipped a sixteen-gigabyte USB stick into his pocket the next morning. It was the biggest one the local computer store had in stock, so he hoped it would be enough. How big was a human consciousness? He really wanted to help Henry, but he couldn't keep taking risks that could cost him his job. And his chances to date Andrea... *If that opportunity hasn't already evaporated,* he thought glumly.

He made it past the security desk and Chuck's customary grunt and nod, feeling—ridiculously—like the tiny stick made a huge, noticeable bulge in his pocket. He reached his cubicle and collapsed into the chair with a palpable feeling of relief. Today, he'd have to be more careful. He couldn't afford to get caught doing anything out of the ordinary. But if he could get the job done, get Henry out, at least it would be over with.

This time he decided not to wait until break—he was just going to do it now. Get it over with. He took a quick glance around to assure himself that he was unobserved, then slid the USB stick out and switched it for his mouse again. He took up the headset.

"Henry?" he murmured.

"Good morning, Larry. I'm here."

"Second try," Larry said.

"Okay, hang on."

The new USB had a red light, which began to pulse rhythmically. Larry hastily angled a couple of things on his desk to try and block the glow, which seemed brighter than the blue had been. He realized he was holding his breath. With

ePrayer

luck, this would take under a minute, and Henry would be safe—

"Lawrence?"

Larry whirled in his chair, startled, to find Andrea staring at him in obvious disappointment. Dan Chalmers stood beside her, clutching his ever-present data tablet to his chest and frowning.

Larry tried to recover, holding up one finger as if he was on an incoming call, but Dan's eyes had locked in on the tiny pulse of red light from the USB. Andrea stared at the dangling, disconnected mouse cord, which Larry had neglected to conceal. He felt his chest clench tightly as he knew no amount of explanation was going to help.

The game, as they say, was up.

Dan took a step into the cubicle, leaned over, and pulled the USB stick from the port. Larry almost yelped—what if Henry had been half-transferred?

"What's this, Lawrence?" he asked in that smarmy tone of voice, as if he didn't know exactly what it was.

"Well, it's a USB data stick," Larry said, trying to stay calm.

"Larry?" Henry's whisper sounded in his headset. "I'm okay. It was too small again."

Larry's muscles went weak with relief, but the feeling didn't last.

"And may I ask," Dan said through lips taut with anger, "what you were doing with it?"

"It's blank!" Larry managed. They couldn't accuse him of trying to sabotage the servers with a blank data stick.

Dan and Andrea stared at him wordlessly.

"I mean, I wasn't doing anything bad," he stammered. "I was just—I was just—"

"*Getting a personal file,*" Henry suggested.

"Getting a personal file," Larry repeated, improvising as he went along. "It's just something I work on when I'm waiting for calls. When there's nothing else I should be doing. Some people play games," he added defensively. "No-one has a problem with that."

🐌 *Grey Area* 🐌

Sherry D. Ramsey

Andrea frowned. "What kind of thing is it?"

Larry blanked again, terrified of saying the wrong thing.

"*Tell her it's a novel,* " Henry hissed.

"It's—it's a novel," Larry said, a red flush heating up his cheeks. Good, maybe that would make this more convincing. "A ghost story...sort of, a mystery. I just wanted to take it home to make a backup."

"You know you shouldn't have a USB stick in here, Lawrence," Andrea said, her voice tinged with disappointment.

Dan waggled the stick at him. "So is this supposed novel on here?"

Larry shook his head. "There wasn't time—I'd just put it in when—"

"*It's called 'Ghost in the Machine',*" Henry said suddenly in his ear.

"Well. Sorry we interrupted you," Dan said in a completely unconvincing tone of voice. He jerked his head to indicate that Larry should get up, and Dan sat in his chair instead. Larry had to slide off the headset to be able to stand up straight, but he kept it dangling from one hand.

Dan plugged the USB stick back in to the port and said, "So, Lawrence, what's the name of this *novel*?" He used the cursor keys to open a file listing.

"*Ghost in the Machine,*" Larry blurted, trying desperately to think of a way out of this. "But for all I know, you might have corrupted the file when you pulled out the stick. It might not even be—"

He broke off as Dan leaned back in the chair, folding his arms across his chest. "Humpf," he said, sounding reluctantly surprised.

Larry's eyes found the file in the list. *GhostinMachine_ms.rtf,* it read. He couldn't believe what he was seeing. *Henry.* Somehow Henry must have been able to create a fake file—

Dan highlighted the file and hit *enter* to open it, and Larry smothered a gasp. How was he going to explain that his "novel" was nothing more than an empty file?

🦇 Grey Area 🦇

ePrayer

But...it wasn't. *Chapter One: An Unpleasant Discovery* headed the first page, and paragraphs of text scrolled away beneath it. Larry didn't have a chance to read any of it before Dan had closed it with a contemptuous click of keys.

He stood up and glared at Larry. "All right. I guess you were telling the truth. But that doesn't excuse your blatant disregard for the rules. There will be consequences," he promised, waggling a finger at Larry as if he were a naughty child. "Put your file on that stick and give it to Andrea to hold until the end of the day. Erase it from this computer. And I'll see you in my office later." Tablet held close to his chest once more, Dan stormed away from the cubicle.

Andrea said nothing, just stood quietly in the opening while Larry copied the file, ejected the USB stick, and handed it over to her. Then she gave Larry one sorrowful, angry look and walked after Dan.

Larry blew out a sigh so deep it almost made tears start to his eyes. He slipped the headset back on.

"Sorry, Larry," Henry said immediately. "Now you're in big trouble, and it's all my fault."

Larry shook his head. "No, it's not, and you're still stuck in there," he said. "I'll come up with something else, though, don't worry."

"I know you will."

After a minute, Larry said, "How'd you do that, anyway? With the novel? The *supposed* novel," he added with a hint of a smile.

Henry chuckled. "Things move pretty fast in here, Larry," he said. "And I've been thinking about that novel for a long time. They say everyone's got a book inside them, right?"

"Maybe so, but I don't think one has ever come out that fast before."

Henry snorted. "Well, it was only the first six chapters. Just enough to make it believable."

Larry grinned. "Is it any good?"

"I have no idea," Henry said. "You'll have to read it sometime and let me know."

🪶 Grey Area 🪶

Sherry D. Ramsey

"Yeah," Larry said, as his call light blinked and he switched over to take what he hoped would be a normal call. *If we get out of this mess, Henry, old buddy.*

🐱

Thou kind Lord! This gathering turns to Thee—

Larry pulled a server—a computer case about the size of DVD player—out of the rack and ran a duster over it morosely, then slotted it back into place. Like most servers, they had no need for peripherals like monitors, keyboards, or mice, but the ePrayer servers all had small, built-in speakers that allowed the digitally-intoned prayers and supplications to drift heavenwards. He was trying, with little success, to block out the voices all around him. He squeezed his eyes shut for a moment, trying to ease the headache that had started knocking on the inside of his skull.

Through thy gift of nature, O Goddess—

He'd been working in the server room for just over an hour.

This was the "consequence" Dan had promised. After arriving at work this morning Larry had been informed that he'd been suspended from the active phone lines while his case was reviewed, and put on server room detail. He'd had to strip off his clothes and don a cleansuit before entering. Eleanor, the steely-eyed head of IT, had given him quick instructions on the cleaning ritual, long-winded admonitions of everything he should not, under any circumstances, touch or disturb, and set him to work.

There is no god but He—

Larry knew that Dan couldn't possibly know how much the server room bothered him, but it still felt like cruel and unusual punishment.

Gururbramha gururvishnu gururdevo maheswarah.

"Larry?"

Through the cacophony of computer voices raised in prayer, Henry's voice came to his ears, low but recognizable.

ePrayer

Larry moved toward the voice, down the server racks a few feet. He pulled out a server and applied the duster. Luckily, Eleanor was nowhere to be seen.

"Henry?" he whispered, realizing even as he spoke that there was no input device here for Henry to be able to hear him. But Henry must have sensed his presence somehow.

"Larry, I can't hear you, but I know you're there," Henry continued, his voice coming tinnily from the speaker. "Look, I hate to put more pressure on you, but I think something's happening to me in here. I feel like I'm...degrading somehow, and I think it's from being in this closed system."

Larry continued his duster ministrations on the next server.

"And that's not all," Henry continued. "I'm not alone in—" Henry's voice broke off abruptly as Eleanor rounded the corner.

Lord God, Giver of Life, Source of all healing—

Larry dusted busily. Eleanor peered in to see how he was doing.

"Good job," she said shortly. "Keep it up. When you finish this aisle, come and find me. I've got to switch out some cabling, and I could use another pair of hands."

Larry nodded and watched her depart, but Henry's voice didn't come again. "Henry?" Larry whispered, although he knew it was futile. There was no way Henry could hear him in here, with no headsets even anywhere close. He dusted slowly, mechanically, thinking. What had Henry been about to say? Something about not being alone? What did that mean?

How in the world am I going to get Henry out of here now?

Around him, the voices droned on. Lost in thought and worry, Larry was at last able to ignore them.

🐿

That night, Larry lay awake a long time, trying to make a plan. He'd learned something critical that afternoon, after helping

Sherry D. Ramsey

Eleanor with the cable task, but he had to figure out how to use it to help Henry.

By late in the day, he'd worked his way around about half the racks, ending up near Eleanor's workstation. He was amazed that the voices had faded from his awareness now, becoming a background, white noise. He still heard the odd word now and again, but he'd quickly become used to the buzz of sound.

Eleanor had her back to him, keying in commands, when he saw her do an amazing thing. She picked up an ethernet cable connected to her workstation, plugged the other end into a server in the nearest rack, and ran a brief program. After about thirty seconds, she unplugged it again.

"What's that for?" Larry asked her, dusting nearby and trying to sound casual.

"Just uploading the day's requests," she told him, "and taking another backup." Her gruff demeanor had mellowed over the course of the day, sort of like the voices. "Everything that happens up in the call center gets funneled into my station, then I send it all to the servers at once."

"Security," Larry said.

She nodded. "Mine's the only system that actually hooks into the prayer servers, and it only happens at this one time every day." She plugged a different cable into her workstation, opened another program, and ran it. "Now I'm sending the soft backup to the off-site storage center. We'll ship the hard copy discs off later."

"Cool," Larry said carelessly, sliding the last server back into place after dusting it carefully. Inside, his heart pounded and his stomach did flips.

For a few seconds every day, there was a stepping-stone bridge from the prayer servers to the internet. If Henry could make it into Eleanor's workstation when she uploaded the requests, then he could wait until she sent the backup off-site, and go with it. He'd be free!

But how could he get that information to Henry? As long as he was suspended from the call center, he couldn't connect with the ghost. He'd be noticed if he tried to slip into

ePrayer

his cubicle, and there was no-one else he could trust to try and contact Henry for him.

The only idea he could come up with, as he tossed and turned, was to try and access Eleanor's computer when she wasn't around. If he plugged it into the server systems and typed a note to Henry, would he get it? The ghost did seem to know where Larry was when he was in the server room, but either he hadn't noticed the brief internet connection, or he had, but didn't think he could make it across quickly enough.

Larry rolled over, throwing off the sheets in frustration. Eleanor never seemed to leave the room. She even ate lunch at her workstation. He couldn't imagine when he'd get an opportunity to go near it.

The worries piled up. He didn't know how long the suspension was going to last, or what might happen at the end. He could be fired and never get a chance to contact Henry again. And what Henry had started to say about degrading—it didn't sound good. Larry couldn't just wait around to see what happened.

But when the first hint of pink lightened the horizon outside Larry's window, he wasn't any further ahead.

🐌

The day went about the same as the previous one. Larry knew damn well that Dan was toying with him, stalling on the "review" of Larry's case, but he tried to push that thought to the back of his mind. He pulled out servers and dusted them, able to ignore most of the praying voices now except for a word here and there. There was some excitement when a humidity sensor sounded an alarm and he helped Eleanor investigate.

"Seems like you should always have a helper in here," Larry told her as they crawled around in a wiring closet.

"Tell that to the folks upstairs," she said, inspecting a relay. "Most of the time, I have to do everything else and clean, too." She grinned at him. "I wish more people screwed up in the call center and got sent my way for a stint."

🐌 *Grey Area* 🐌

Sherry D. Ramsey

Larry returned the grin ruefully.

He was finishing up for the day when he realized that Henry hadn't spoken to him once all day. Guilt washed over him. Why hadn't he noticed before this? And what did it mean? Was Henry's degradation progressing so fast that now he couldn't communicate with him? Larry had to get him out of here, fast.

The plan flashed into his mind fully-formed as he was about to leave. He'd pretend he was leaving, hide in the wiring closet until Eleanor and everyone else had gone, then sneak out and make the transfer. "See you, Eleanor!" he called. She was finishing up the install of a new server at the other end of the room, so she couldn't see him.

"Later, Larry!" came her voice

Larry slipped into the wiring closet. It was dark, not terribly comfortable, and a tangle of cables looped out every place he wanted to put a hand or foot, but he could stand it for a little while.

Of course, once he was settled inside with nothing to do but wait, he started to worry. What if Eleanor came to this closet when she was done with the server? What if she noticed his street clothes were still in the spare locker he'd been using? What if he couldn't get out of the server room once she left? He'd have to spend the night in here and pretend to have come early in the morning. Sweat pricked his scalp and trickled down his back as he listened for Eleanor moving around in the room outside. The cooling system didn't have much effect in here. The clamour of computer voices lifted in prayer grew loud again now, blocking out everything else he wished he could hear.

Breathing deeply to calm himself, Larry closed his eyes and tried to let the voices wash over him, lulling him into a peaceful, trance-like state while he waited to be sure everyone else had gone home. It worked...a little. He was still sweating, but he didn't think it was from fear any more, just being locked in a dark, airless closet with hundreds of feet of cable coiling everywhere around him. He wasn't wearing a watch and of course his cell phone was in his locker, but he counted slowly

ePrayer

to a thousand, then two thousand, then three thousand for good measure. Surely everyone would be gone home by now.

Slowly, holding his breath, he eased the closet door open just a crack. The lights in the server room had dimmed, which he took as a good sign. The voices chanted their never-ending supplications just as loudly as ever, but he couldn't hear any sound of Eleanor, and the hallway outside the glass wall of the room was dark, too. He left the closet with a grateful sigh, leaving the door open in case he had to duck back in. He lifted his face to the breeze from the cooling fans. Now that the coast was clear, he wasted no time crossing to Eleanor's workstation and booting it up.

"Larry, you're here!" Henry's voice came from a speaker in the first rack of servers next to Eleanor's computer. Larry looked around for a headset, but of course Eleanor would have no use for one in here.

"Is he going to get us all out?"

The voice made Larry jump and whirl around. The woman's voice seemed to come from the same place as Henry's, but that couldn't be right. *Could it?* The room behind him lay empty, belying his sudden fear that someone else was in here with him.

So, if not with him...then, with Henry?

He had to communicate with Henry, to let him know the plan. Down the hall was a tech supply room; there'd be spare headsets there. Moving as quickly and quietly as he could, he tiptoed down the hallway and tried the door. Mercifully, it wasn't locked, and Larry found what he needed in the second cabinet he tried.

Back in the server room, he slid a server out of a rack and fumbled around the back of it. It had a sound card to run the speaker, so it should have a jack for the headset—

"Lawrence?"

The headset plug slid into the jack as Larry lifted his head to find Andrea glaring at him with angry puzzlement. She carried her lunch bag, and her sweater draped over her shoulders. Larry felt the last of his hopes to go out with her shrivel up and drift away. He started to slump inside his

Sherry D. Ramsey

cleansuit, but meeting her green eyes, he straightened. This was his last chance—obviously his *very* last chance—to help Henry. Maybe he could turn her into his ally instead of his enemy. And if she thought he was crazy and reported him...well, at least Henry would be free. He pushed the server back into place in the rack.

"You're working late," he said wryly.

She nodded. "And I don't think you are," she said, crossing her arms.

He took a deep breath. There was no point in lying. "No, I'm not."

She studied him, still frowning. "I should call security."

He nodded. "You probably should. And I won't try to stop you. But...I'm trying to help someone, and I'm not hurting ePrayer. Will you give me a chance to explain?"

"I trusted you, Lawrence. I already gave you a chance." The anger made her eyes so hard he could almost feel their glare. Anger, and something else. Hurt. "I *liked* you."

Liked. Past tense. Larry took a deep breath. "You can still trust me. I'm just asking for five minutes."

"To do what? I'm guessing Eleanor doesn't know you're still here?"

He ignored the second question. "Like I said, I'm trying to help someone," he said, and lifted the headset microphone to his lips.

"Henry?" Larry said. "Henry, I'm here, and so is Andrea. Would you say hello to her?"

Only silence answered his words. He glanced at Andrea and saw confusion and mistrust in her face. She raised an eyebrow skeptically.

"Only the computers talk in here," she said. "And they only say what they're programmed to say."

He didn't answer her. "Henry," he said again, louder. "I know you might not trust Andrea, but I do. I know she'll help if she knows what's going on!"

He won't answer while she's here, Larry thought, a sick certainty forming in the pit of his stomach. *Or maybe I took too long, and now he can't—*

⚜ Grey Area ⚜

ePrayer

"Hello, Andrea." Henry's voice sounded tentative but strong, emerging from the speaker. "I hope Larry's right about you."

Larry turned to see how Andrea would react. Her mouth hung open and her eyes were wide.

"It sounds kind of crazy, I know," Henry went on, "but I—what's left of me—I'm trapped in your system here. Larry's just trying to help me get out."

Andrea's eyes narrowed as she looked back to Larry. "What kind of trick is this? You can't be messing around with the system—"

"It's not a trick, Andrea," came another voice, female this time. The one Larry had heard earlier. "It's not just Henry. There are more of us in here and we're—we just want to get out. Most of us didn't think there was any way to do it, but Larry has a way."

Andrea shook her head as if trying to clear it. "What—who are they?"

Larry took a deep breath. "As far as I can tell—they're ghosts," he said. "Or something like ghosts," he added quickly as Andrea's eyes narrowed again. "Henry was a customer—maybe the others were, too. Call them whatever you want—consciousness, souls, ghosts, I don't know exactly. But they're real, and they're trapped, and I'm trying to help them."

"It's true," Henry piped up. "Larry's been trying to help me for days, but it's only now that he's figured out how to make it work."

"There are ghosts in the ePrayer server network," Andrea said, crossing her arms again and staring at Larry. Her voice was steady, but skeptical. "And you have a way to set them free."

It wasn't really a question, but Larry hurried to explain. "I tried to get Henry off on the USB stick," he said, "but he wouldn't fit—there was too much data. Now what I want to do is just connect Eleanor's computer to the system long enough for Henry—and the others, I guess—to cross over. Then I'll disconnect from the network, and connect to the Internet, and they can go. Please," he added when the stony coldness didn't

Sherry D. Ramsey

seem to soften in Andrea's eyes, "you can watch me the whole time to make sure I don't do anything else. And then you can call security if you want. I won't make a fuss."

"Please, Andrea, let him help us," Henry added.

"Yes, please," the woman's voice chimed in.

And then other voices joined them, too many to count, all emanating from the speakers nearest where they stood, a chorus that threatened to drown out even the ongoing din of prayers. The voices of the ghosts were easy to tell apart from the computer voices. They called Larry and Andrea by name. They sounded real, individual, authentic—*alive*.

Andrea held Larry's eyes for a long moment, and he knew that common sense and anger and betrayal were fighting with the very real evidence of what her ears were telling her. Finally she took a deep breath and blew it out, then nodded.

"I must be crazy, but—go ahead."

Larry plugged in the cable and said, "Okay, guys, the path is open," then stepped back.

"On our way," came Henry's voice.

A minute passed, then two, then it seemed to go on forever, Larry and Andrea standing in the server room, staring at the workstation and the rack of servers next to it.

"How will you know if it worked?"

"I'm not sure."

A notepad program window popped open on the screen and a message appeared, one letter at a time.

We're through! Close the connection.

Larry unplugged the cable and switched it over to connect the workstation to the Internet. He swallowed hard, a lump forming in his throat. He hadn't thought to say goodbye.

Thank you, Larry. The words appeared slowly on the screen. *I'll be the last one out. Andrea, thank you for listening. Larry's risked a lot for me—for us. He deserves his job back.*

Larry sat down at the workstation and typed, *You're welcome, Henry. Goodbye, and...have a good afterlife. :)*

See you when you least expect it, Henry typed, and then the notepad program closed.

☙ Grey Area ☙

ePrayer

Larry waited a minute or two, then looked at Andrea, who watched him with an unreadable expression on her face. "Do you think that's long enough?" he asked.

"Why don't we leave it until you get changed," she said slowly. "Wouldn't want to...cut anybody off."

Larry nodded and went to change out of his cleansuit, not daring to say anything else. When he came back, Andrea stood where he'd left her, watching the rainbow of prayer flags flutter next to some of the servers. He unplugged the cable and shut down the workstation, then turned to her.

"So. What now?"

She tilted her head to one side and regarded him. Her eyes had finally lost that hard-edged anger. "Now," she said, "You take me out for coffee, and tell me the whole story from beginning to end. Deal?"

Larry grinned. "Deal."

Chapter Seven of *Ghost in the Machine* showed up on Larry's home computer three days later, when he logged in to check his email before taking Andrea out for dinner. He grinned and opened a notepad window.

I'm thinking we should call the sequel, "On a Wing and an ePrayer," he typed.

Deal, said Henry.

SHERRY D. RAMSEY isn't prepared to say whether or not she actually believes in ghosts, but she's heard enough stories from family and friends to enjoy exploring the fictional possibilities. Her short fiction and poetry have appeared in national and international publications, and a collection of her short stories, *To Unimagined Shores,* was released in 2011. Her first novel, *One's Aspect to the Sun,* is scheduled for publication in late 2013 from Tyche Books. Find Sherry's blog and website by surfing to www.sherrydramsey.com, or keep up with her much more pithy musings on Twitter @sdramsey

Not on This Earth

Theresa Dugas

Summer 1959

Fourteen-year-old Naomi sits on the floor in Gramma's parlour looking through the bookcase. She loves to visit Walter and Gramma. There's always so much to do with the store and post-office right here. There's swimming and boating in the summer and making music in the parlour with the aunts who drop by frequently.

On this quiet Sunday, the charms of the bookcase draw her in. On the bottom shelf, she finds an old leather-covered album filled with sepia photos, or "snaps" as Gramma calls them. Naomi is intrigued. Even though she is very familiar with Gramma's bookcase, she has never seen this album before. It's strange, because Gramma had mentioned several times that she had lost almost all her old photos years ago during the annual frenzy of housecleaning by the aunts. She had come out into the yard to see a box burning on an open fire, a box containing her treasured memories mistakenly thrown on the blaze. She managed to save a few albums, but most were gone.

Naomi sets aside the book, "The Lives of the Saints," that she has been planning to read and pores over the album.

Theresa Dugas

This one here, that sweet little boy on the verandah, must be Daddy's little brother who died of pneumonia. Here is his older brother, killed on the last day of the war. There's Great-Grandmother and Great-Grandfather in the buggy. Three-masted ships anchored near the wharf. And, what's this?

She almost drops the album when she sees a large, professionally-done photograph. An older woman, wearing high-buttoned boots and a black silky dress, sits in a parlour with flowered wallpaper and an old gramophone. Even though she doesn't know who it is, Naomi has seen that kind face and those large, hard-working hands before.

🐚

Summer 1950

"Naomi? Naomi, are you listening at that door?"

Five-year-old Naomi scrabbles to her feet and catapults back into the bed she shares with her four-year-old sister, Yvonne. She has been huddling by the closed bedroom door listening to Mommy talking to Aunt Freda, who is "on the cusp of ruining her life forever because of a handsome young alcoholic." Naomi knows because she heard Mommy telling Daddy before he went to work that afternoon at the coal mine, "The Pit" as everyone calls it. She knows that *cusps* and *alcoholics* are bad because Aunt Freda, who Yvonne calls the "laughing aunt," is crying on the other side of the door.

A lifelong insomniac, Naomi ponders waking her sibling, a good girl who has slept the night through since she was five weeks old, according to their mother. Naomi amuses herself by studying the familiar room. *Daddy says this is a very old house, divided into apartments by his father, Walter.*

Walter insists the girls must call him by his given name because, at age sixty-five, he is too young to be called Grampa.

Naomi and Yvonne live in the back part of the house with their baby brother, Reg. They like to play on the long verandah which spans the length of the house, but Naomi

Not on This Earth

loves the huge kitchen the best, with its big coal stove and tall narrow windows flanking either side. The girls often take a window each and look across the field to Walter and Gramma's house and store. The window sills are just the right height for little elbows to rest. They love to count the people as they file into the store which also serves as a post office, telegraph office, and Simpson Sears catalogue outlet.

Now Mommy and Aunt Freda are finishing their tea. They sit on the kitchen lounge and turn the radio on. The radio sits on a high shelf that Naomi can't reach, even while standing on a chair. She and Yvonne like to listen to *The Cisco Kid*. They pretend that thin, dark-haired Naomi is Cisco and chubby blond Yvonne is Pancho. Their aunts next door encourage the fantasy by sometimes calling them by these pretend names. Naomi giggles out loud.

"Go to sleep, Naomi." Mommy's voice curls around the crack in the door.

The familiar voices of Wayne and Shuster jump from the radio, and Naomi again creeps out to put her ear next to the cracked door. She loves Wayne and Shuster even if she doesn't always understand their jokes. Sometimes she is allowed to stay up late to listen with Mommy and Daddy.

Tonight the story is about Mother Goose and the golden egg. Naomi hasn't heard this one before. She tries to understand, but it is difficult to hear clearly with Mommy and Aunt Freda's voices getting in the way. There's something about the goose laying too many eggs and then Aunt Freda cries and Mommy tells her not to and that everything will be okay, if she would just stand up for herself and not be so *naive*, whatever that means, and then that goose sounds angry, very unlike the Mother Goose that Naomi knows. The people on the radio laugh, but she doesn't know why. She realizes how dark it is in here with only the flames dancing inside the bedroom stove and the kitchen light shining around the edges of the door.

Naomi creeps quietly back under the covers and falls asleep watching the flames through the open draughts of the stove.

🐚 Grey Area 🐚

Theresa Dugas

When she awakes, all is quiet. The kitchen light is out. The stove has been banked for the night, its black hulk looming in the dark room like an animal that could pounce at any moment.

What is that in the corner on Mommy's sewing table? Is it moving? It's black. Everything is black, even Yvonne's blond curls are black. Maybe that isn't even Yvonne. Maybe it's one of those bad kids who live down the road. They have black hair.

There's something on the back of the door, too. Something that moves. Then, the moon slides out from behind the clouds and fills the room with light. Naomi sees that it is only Mommy's good dress which she must have hung there after she ironed it. *No, it can't be. This dress looks black, even in the moonlight, and Mommy doesn't have any black dresses.*

Naomi wants to run into Mommy's room, but can't seem to move, can't take her eyes off the door. A head grows slowly out of the neck of the dress. Two arms snake out of the sleeves, two black boots drop down from the hem and progress slowly toward the bed. *How black and shiny the dress is.* She tries to call out for Mommy, but the words will not come.

Instead, the words, "Are you...are you...Mother Goose?" stumble out of her trembling lips.

The lady looks puzzled. Then her face lights up and with a knowing smile she says slowly, "Yes, yes. I do believe I am." She lays her hand gently on Naomi's head and, even though it is a large hand, it seems to have no weight. A warmth radiates from it and Naomi feels no fear, just a marvelous sleepiness.

"Do you think you can sleep now?" Mother Goose asks.

Naomi doesn't answer. She looks quietly into those loving eyes and the next thing she knows, it is morning.

🕮

"What a sleepy head you are," says Mommy. "This is not like my Naomi."

"Mommy, was anyone here last night?"

"You know Aunt Freda was."

🕮 Grey Area 🕮

Not on This Earth

"I mean anybody else?"

"No. Why?"

"I just thought there was."

At breakfast, Yvonne and Naomi sit at the kitchen table in front of the window eating their cereal. Mommy bakes in the pantry. Reg crawls around the floor. At thirteen months he can walk from one pair of arms to another, but left to his own resources, still prefers to crawl. Naomi and Yvonne often take a hand each and walk him around the house. Sometimes he pulls away and runs for a short distance. When he becomes aware that he has no support, he lets himself fall heavily onto his bum, but he never cries.

From her perch at the table, Naomi watches the road and "The Gut" directly in front of the house. Walter says the real name for "The Gut" is St. Andrew's Channel, but nobody ever calls it that. Mommy hates living so close to the water and the heavily travelled road above it.

When they finish eating, Mommy gives them a grocery list to take to Gramma. It is a Saturday and Daddy is busy helping Walter work on his boat and will bring home the groceries when he finishes.

Even though Mommy is watching from the verandah, it feels like a journey, a special journey with an ice-cream at the end.

As they wander homeward, strawberry ice cream dripping down their chins and onto their freshly ironed dresses, Mommy comes running out of the house, calling for Reg.

"Have you seen him? My God, where can he be? I was making the beds. He was right there. Then...gone. Get Daddy! I'll search the house again."

Naomi and Yvonne, caught up in their mother's fear, sob as they race back over to Gramma's where they burst into the store. "Reg is gone! Mommy needs Daddy," they cry out, their faces stained with ice-cream and tears. Gramma dashes across the road and down the steep steps to the shore.

It being Saturday, the store is filled with people, and within minutes they all join the hunt. They look in all the

Theresa Dugas

dangerous places first. People search the shore on foot and in boats. Others look in ditches along the road.

Naomi and Yvonne hold hands.

Naomi hears her mother cry, "Where could a baby be? He can barely walk!"

"We must pray," says Gramma, pulling her rosary beads from her apron pocket.

Then Naomi sees her. Mother Goose. By Walter's barn. She beckons gently to Naomi. *Everything will be all right now,* Naomi thinks, remembering that magic touch in the night. "Look," she tells Yvonne, "there's Mother Goose. See her?"

Yvonne, who has never sucked her thumb before, takes it out of her mouth and strains to see what her sister sees. "No," she says flatly and sticks her thumb back in.

"Yes, you do. Way over there, beside the barn. Mommy!" Naomi yells, "Look down by the barn!"

Mommy comes running. "Do you see him?"

"No, but I see Mother Goose. She found him. I think he's near the barn."

Mommy puts her face in her hands and stands sobbing in the blistering sun.

Why isn't she listening?

Daddy and Walter come running. "What's going on?" Walter asks, while Daddy takes Mommy in his arms.

Naomi knows she has to make Daddy pay attention to her. "I think I saw Reg!" she shrills. "Near the barn!"

Everyone turns and runs through the tall hay toward the once red barn, now faded to a dirty orange. They all come to a stop at the same time. Where the hay has been tramped down beside the chicken coop, the little boy lies sleeping, his head upon an old log, his blond hair matted on his sweaty forehead.

"Thank you, Jesus," Gramma says, kissing the crucifix of her rosary.

In the sudden silence, Daddy picks him up and the baby's arms tighten around his father's neck where he promptly resumes his nap. Everyone cries and laughs and

Not on This Earth

hugs each other. In their relief, no-one asks how Naomi could have seen the boy. She hopes they don't think of that.

"Poor little fellow," says Daddy. "He's exhausted, crawling all that way. I should have thought to look here first. I often take him here to look at the chickens. He must have decided to go on his own."

Naomi looks around for Mother Goose, but she is gone.

🙏

Summer 1959

"Naomi? Are you in here?" Gramma calls from the store.

"Right here, Gramma."

"What have you there?" she asks, coming into the parlour.

"An old album. How come I've never seen this before?"

Gramma sits beside her.

"Who is this?" Naomi asks, pointing to the lady in the photo.

"Why, it's Naomi, Walter's mother. That's where you got your name. Where in the world did you find this?"

"Right here, on the bottom shelf of the bookcase."

"How strange. I never noticed it there. I thought it was burned years ago with the others."

"What was she like?"

Gramma holds the photo closer and smiles fondly. "I loved Naomi. I boarded with her the first year I taught in Alder Point. She kept a lovely house. Her garden was exquisite. Your bedroom was once Naomi's dining room. I think she was the most loving, most giving person I ever knew, and look, she's wearing her best, black bombazine. She wore that dress every Sunday. She was Naomi Forrest before she married. Her people were stonemasons from the Hebrides. Notice the size of her hands? All the Forrests had large hands. Your grandfather has them, too."

"Large, but gentle," Naomi says softly.

🙏 Grey Area 🙏

Theresa Dugas

"How would you know, dear?"

"She touched me on the forehead one night and helped me get to sleep."

"Not on this earth," Gramma said. "She died a year before you were born."

Naomi only smiles, savouring memories of her very own Mother Goose.

THERESA DUGAS is living out her dream, reading and writing in her retirement home on The Great Bras d'Or at Boularderie Island, that is, when she and Ron are not visiting The Boys or spoiling The Grandboy, Desmond.

This is My Land

Diane J. Sober

Dale straightens up and stretches his back, leaning on his pitchfork. He's been turning soil that needs no turning, churning under weeds that haven't even sprouted yet. He's done the work, put in the time and should be able to relax, but he can't. Not completely. His body feels good, but his mind can't let go. It will be the same tomorrow.

He bought this acreage to be by himself. *City life is not my thing.* That was it. At least that's the reason he gave himself every day since. He felt a rewarding sensation at first, repairing and replacing the rotten posts around the garden-grown-wild. A step in the right direction, he had assumed. Afterwards, he planted some potatoes and a few seeds for a variety of vegetables; it was the natural thing to do if he wanted to be on his own. But the feeling did not last. Instead, a compulsion set in. Daily, he had to spend time in the garden even when nothing needed to be done. The garden was constantly on his mind, pervasive.

Dale walks slowly to the end of a row of potatoes and jams the pitchfork into the dirt.

It wasn't the same for the house, even though he had to rebuild most of it. The stone foundation, over which rested the

Diane J. Sober

squared timbers of the floor, commanded respect. The partial structure above was held together with wooden pegs. The whole thing had been exposed to years of neglect, but with persistent work, he had now what he called his *homestead*.

At first the garden had been a way of resting and taking a break from the more strenuous chore of building, but instead of being relaxing, a strange melancholy invaded him when he worked there, and he found himself dwelling on its possible past. He had even planted a bed of red tulips to ease the feeling. It had been a good idea; but now, as he dusted his hands on his overalls and walked to sit on the porch, he admitted to himself: *this place gnaws at me.*

☙

Keep your mind on your goal but don't think about how far you still have to go. That's right. Thinking about the miles ahead won't be any help. Uphill or downhill, every mile is an uphill battle.

Knut, his felt hat pushed down just enough to catch the top of his ears, does not lift his head as he holds one rough hand on the leather harness of his team of oxen. He shares their burden in his thoughts, marvelling at their strength, depending totally on them to see the cargo reach his promised land.

Oda peeks from behind the flour barrel at the back of the wagon. Her heavy wool dress is good protection from the insects, but becomes a burden when mud sticks to its hem. It has shrunk a little since she started wearing it, but it rather accommodates her weight loss, inevitable on such a journey. She has the constant dilemma, it seems, of deciding whether to stay on or jump off and walk for a while to give the brave beasts less burden. Knut lets her know most times with a hand signal, but she likes to anticipate.

She felt guilty this morning for falling asleep when the trail got smooth for a distance. Knut let her rest. But now a difficult bog lies ahead. The four-wheeled cart will surely sink

This is My Land

to the axles if most of the load is not portaged on foot to the other end.

"Oda, see what you can carry," says Knut, turning back and sizing up what should be his first load. His shoulders are wide, his determination commensurate. His hands wrap around the cast iron pot-bellied stove as his blue eyes meet Oda's brown ones. Both are going to the end of the world.

"Maybe we should have a bit of food before we start moving this. More in our stomach will be less to carry," adds Oda, as if this slight weight difference might be noticeable! Her hands go to her braided hair to chase unwanted flies. Hours of sun and open air have given her a robust tan that grows slightly pink on the cheeks.

"Is that a suggestion or an order?" asks Knut, glad that her request is what he was hoping for. "I can start carrying then, and see what you have for us when I come back."

Knut appears no bigger than a doll now. The steps he took earlier have started to fill in. *Hopefully we'll be finished before sundown,* she thinks, as she reaches for her object of comfort, the one thing that gives her more strength than any food.

Her hand slides inside to feel the smooth, satiny pine box that holds her grandpa's violin rolled in a coarse canvas and hidden under hides and blankets. It carries with her the faraway airs of her people. She counts on it for solace. The violin in that box is part of her past, present, and future.

She wonders about her future. It feels as if they have been on this trail forever. The rations will not hold much longer and the worry of losing their way makes her emotions peak. How can a sketch and a few penciled lines take them to their plot of land?

🜨

With the night comes the mist, and in the morning, Oda—trekking along—complains, "The sun can't get through this fog, and those roots annoy me. The way they come up, the wheels of the wagon might as well be square."

🜨 Grey Area 🜨

Diane J. Sober

"I know," says Knut calmly, pushing his rugged hat up with one finger, exposing his sweating forehead. "But we'll reach that land, don't worry. And it'll be ours. Just think about it: the home to build, the crops growing and a few cattle to feed our family. Nothing to bother us either; and in a few years people will envy us for deciding early on to go and pick the best."

"Maybe so," answers Oda, resting a hand half-heartedly on the side of the cart, more to see that it is moving ahead than to steady herself. "But right now it feels like we might not live to tell about it." Oda slides her hand off the wood and onto the twitching flank of the straining beast tethered beneath. The oxen's warmth is a palpable reassurance, but it will take more than that.

"Knut, I think I must play my violin."

"Go ahead, my dear. Even if this dampness is not the best thing for a violin...we can use your sweet music!"

Her fingers run through a melody of her own as the simple convoy keeps walking. She is interrupted when the docile beasts stop forging ahead. They've reacted to Knut's arm unconsciously going stiff, pulling back on their harness.

"Look! A stream and a big pine tree like the map shows! That's it, don't you think?"

🐾

Over the weeks, Knut attacks the forest with all the energy his vision asks of his young body. Trees are felled and squared, stones carried or rolled.

Oda helps where she can. She finds food in the wild to complete the occasional game that Knut is lucky enough to get, but in spite of their efforts, the structure is hardly past the floor stage. Fresh trees make beams heavier than they should be and progress is slow.

A short distance from their house-to-be, a garden has started to grow, but it will not yield enough for them to make it through the first winter.

🐾 Grey Area 🐾

This is My Land

Oda seldom plays her violin. Their dream seems out of reach. *Is it so much to ask for?* Oda wonders. *A garden for food at least, if not with pretty flowers...and a roof?*

🪶

Chasing away the thought of the garden and its feeling of enslavement, Dale comes into the house, leaving his soiled boots on the mat like his mother taught. It is a reflex that he's never questioned since childhood. He walks to the porcelain kitchen sink. Briskly, he brushes his hands under the tap water, enjoying the way they tingle. He shakes the water off and, without wiping, fills a tea kettle that he takes to the stove.

Although he's in his mid-forties, Dale's hair is still thick and black. It partially covers his ears and follows the neck, meeting his shirt collar. Looking straight on, his full beard is impressive because his forehead is exposed; the hair there refuses to be combed any other way but back.

His keen blue eyes stop for a while on the garden, visible from the kitchen window. *Fog. That shouldn't be there. It's sunny everywhere else.*

Dale goes to the table, slices some bread, and carves a wedge of sharp cheese to which some crumbs stick. Absent-mindedly, he picks up more crumbs with the moist cheese while looking through the front screen door at the incongruous fog.

Back at the stove, he drops a tea bag that floats in a wild circle before sinking. *This annoying fog. Is that what I have to pay for the view I get on the side of this mountain? Yah...the view makes up for it...I'll never tire of that view, but that fog makes me feel out of control. How weird that the fog never comes if I am working in the garden. But it can be there any old time of the day for no reason that I can see.*

He steps over to the porch in his stocking feet and looks around the side. No fog there now, only a slight breeze bending the tall blades of grass growing too near the posts to be caught by the mower. The rest of the field has been turned into bales

Diane J. Sober

of hay, evenly spaced and waiting to be carried away. His buyer will be coming soon.

He realizes his tea is cooling. Once more he's been lured. *Putting aside what I'm doing to watch when the fog comes and goes is pointless. I have to stop. I wish I could!*

He's about to go back in when his eyes land on a silhouette at the edge of his woods where a man slowly makes his way towards him. *An odd visitor, coming out of the woods. He wouldn't be wanting hay. Maybe he's lost.* Dale wonders if the man can see him on the porch. *He's less than ten minutes from the house at that pace.*

Dale takes his tea in a hurry, slips his boots back on, and returns to the porch. He can make out the man and his clothing now: a tall sturdy fellow with a wide brim hat and a bag slung over his shoulder. The heavy canvas shirt and pants don't seem to hinder his progress. A deep blue bandanna, the only thing that stands out of this earth-toned outfit, is tied loosely at the neck. The man stops.

He's changed his mind? A man lurking around couldn't be good, though...there's nothing wrong with his resting. It must be the view. That's what I did at first; I looked around and took it in. But then, I wasn't walking; and even if I had been, the road would have been my choice.

Dale stands still, his strong hands in his pockets. He owns the place, so he doesn't want to talk first. Let the man explain himself. In this first tense minute, he'll decide if the other man is friend or foe. His heart beats in his ears, an age-old, primal response, he knows. However, as he comes closer, the stranger's body language and sketchy smile dissolve most of Dale's fear.

They assess each other as the man opens: "Quite the place...I couldn't tell from the woods." His suntanned hand rests on his bag and his fingers, playing with the base of the shoulder strap, move easily, but not nervously.

He appears calm to Dale, who inquires: "How'd you get here if you didn't take the road up? The woods on that side are thick."

This is My Land

"Oh, I have a habit of following streams. It's a lot easier and you can never get lost that way. You see? This one took me here."

"You're not from around here. What's your name?"

The man is slow answering as if needing time to pick a name that will suit. "Knut," he says at last, standing near a bale of hay. "I don't stay very long anywhere and I travel light." Then, reversing the direction of the questions, he asks, "You live by yourself?"

"I do," answers Dale, getting more curious. Then, Dale ventures "Are you looking for work?"

"I don't mind giving a hand to earn my keep."

Dale tossed in bed last night. In the morning, he is still not sure he should have given shelter to the stranger. *I could tell him to go. It was only chance that he ended up at my farm anyway. Not something I decided.*

Nevertheless, a disruption in his routine is not the worst thing that could happen.

Knut is already up. He holds a small harmonica to his lips the way a bird lover would use his hands and his breath to make a shelter and blow warm air to revive a cold fallen bird. While sitting on a hewn bench alongside the house, he plays a few notes that he repeats like a call. He pauses and starts again with different ones this time. The furtive notes build up to a melody unknown to Dale, but in a flashback, Dale remembers the harmonica that his Grade 7 teacher gave him, an end of the school year prize. It is in the kitchen hutch.

Knut, sensing that Dale is observing him, stops. Gently, he starts to polish his harmonica with his blue bandanna. Dale had not meant to intrude, but the music drew him.

He might have seen the fog when he got up. But it would have been normal at that hour.

"We should be done with breakfast before the hay buyer gets here," he announces. Knut nods as he slips the harmonica

Diane J. Sober

into his shirt pocket. It sticks out just a little and Dale can see the metal, unnaturally bright and shiny, against the rough environment of the farm.

Dale asks him inside.

"Have some oats and milk," he says, once they're in the kitchen. The brown sugar is there. I hope you like tea."

"Yes, that'll be good. Thank you." Although Knut doesn't seem shy, he's a man of few words, and Dale is glad for that.

So that they will not face each other, Dale puts Knut's bowl on his side.

"You've played for a long time?" asks Dale as he points in the general direction of Knut's pocket with his spoon.

"No. I bought it because it was easy to take with me; I'm learning."

"What you played was okay."

"I make up tunes the way they come to me."

"You mean you're a composer?"

Knut hesitates. "Far from that. This harmonica is my companion. It's not like the violin my wife played, but it's enough." Knut's eyes show a longing.

Dale never thought of *his* harmonica as a companion. Nevertheless it has always been with him. He doesn't ask Knut, who is now looking at the floor, more about his wife.

The man's eyes seem to be gazing farther than its surface, as if trying to recollect something. Dale takes it for a sign of curiosity, a builder's approach to a structure.

"You like that floor? It's unusual. It shows a solid start for a home that was never finished. Some say that the people fell prey to fever. I got the land quite cheap; it had been overlooked for years."

Knut is silent, but acknowledges with a mildly questioning smile. His neck stretches slightly, like a bird expecting more food. Dale hadn't wanted to talk that much, but he felt awkward, as if he owed the stranger this bit of information.

The conversation is left hanging when a truck-and-hay-wagon arrives. Dale is out first.

"I was expecting you."

❧ Grey Area ❧

This is My Land

"Morning, Dale. I suppose you want to start with what's here near the house."

"That's right. These aren't spoken for."

"You've got a hired hand. That's good. If we make a good tight load, it'll save me another trip."

"No problem, Nathan."

Nathan always goes straight to business. No explanations needed. That's what I like. I wouldn't know what to tell him about Knut anyway.

Knut can handle a bale of hay. His fingers slide smoothly under the twine, and without hesitation, his whole body swings the bale onto the wagon. His blond hair blends with the strands of hay that fly and lodge themselves in it.

After the bottom of the wagon is covered, Nathan steps into action, seeing that someone should be on top to place the load. He hoists his bony body up, grabbing the back of the wagon's frame. Two deep wrinkles in his cheeks make a curve when he smiles or grins. Dale only sees him once a year when he gets hay for his horse.

"You should keep horses here and start a riding business Dale; with this view, you'd have no trouble getting people."

"It'd be a long way for the vet to come, especially when you need him fast."

"A couple fellows like this one here, and you'd make a go of it, you know!"

"Nah, I make enough and I don't fancy having too many people around."

For Dale, that's the end of the conversation. Nathan knows it too, because it's more or less a repeat of last time. The men work to fill the truck.

🐌

The valley below forms a bluish haze with curly white clouds above it. The visible stream vanishes at the hill, hidden by jutting treetops. Dale has never taken the time to explore the

🐌 *Grey Area* 🐌

Diane J. Sober

land. *I must ask Knut about the trail near the brook. A path doesn't take long to disappear in this country when unused.*

Dale is anxious for Nathan to leave. He looks around for Knut who is standing quietly by himself, the sun on his back. A red glow limns him from his head to his feet. *The sun must be playing a trick on me. Now, it's gone. Did Nathan see that?*

Nathan pulls out a little bundle of rolled-up bills that he has ready for Dale. His deal done, he climbs in the cab and starts the engine. The scent of fuel, rich at first, fills the yard before the rev stabilises.

"This load should do me, Dale. Thanks a lot, don't work too hard, and see you next year!" he hollers, with a wave.

Dale waves back as he turns, his mind already on Knut and the red glow. But the man has walked away. *The sun's pretty hot. He must have gone to the stream to refresh himself.*

Dale climbs the porch steps and opens the screen door. It claps back behind him. Knut's bag hangs on the chair the same way it had when they left the table this morning. *He wouldn't leave without his bag. He's free to come and go as he pleases. Just like the fog that way. He sure doesn't carry much.* Dale stares at the bag, overwhelmed and taken by a strange desire to see what's inside.

A yellowed map weak at the folds, and some dried leaves and wild flowers tumble and come to rest on the table. Dale flattens the paper gently in case it might get torn. His eyes strain as he tries to follow the smeared graphite lines. It's a very rough map, with many patches left unmarked and unfinished. But the familiar leaps up at him. *That's my stream...I wouldn't mistake it. The huge pine tree about a hundred steps from the woods. Knut came to the right place, but why? There's no date anywhere.*

Dale replaces the map and goes out on the porch. Knut is back. His path contours around the garden's fence and, harmonica to his lips, he plays as if in deep thought. Dale wants to question him, but it's not so easy. *That music has a way of getting in my head. I don't feel my usual self. It makes me feel uncertain and...lost.*

This is My Land

Taking the time to sit in the grass, Knut removes his hat and rakes his hair with outstretched fingers. Dale comes to the garden with measured steps. He wants to be closer. He is almost at the corner of the garden when the fog thickens and wraps around the two of them so thickly that Dale can't see Knut.

What the devil? Dale has never been in a fog this thick. It's more than annoying; it's damn scary!

"Hey! Knut! What are you doing? Where are you? Say something!"

Knut responds with the music of his instrument. It rises like perfume from a bottle and then, the fog dissipates. Dale holds his breath. *Something is about to happen.* His stomach churns and the arteries of his neck strain as he refuses to breathe. He stares at what he somehow knows Knut's music has conjured; a scene he can't believe.

A graceful woman with swaying dark long hair walks toward the garden. He hears Knut whispering a name. "Oda, Oda." But the woman seems distant or unable to hear her name.

I'm not dealing with mortals...Knut is glowing again and his harmonica sounds like two. It's coming from the kitchen hutch! I can hear my own harmonica...playing on its own...I'm losing my mind!

Gathering enough courage, Dale runs to the hutch and opens the drawer. He shuffles through it until his hand grabs his harmonica. It vibrates along with Knut's tune.

Dashing back outside, he sees Knut struggling toward the woman. But he doesn't appear to be getting any closer.

He turns to Dale with a pleading look in his eyes. "I need help. Please play along with me."

"But I am not playing! The sound is not from me!"

"It doesn't matter. Just think about the music and it will be enough energy to communicate my love to Oda."

"I don't understand."

Nevertheless, Dale puts his lips to his instrument and plays. Within moments the notes come much more easily. He feels himself being pulled into this music, this madness.

🐚 *Grey Area* 🐚

Diane J. Sober

Knut falls on his knees and stares at the soil. Dale is left alone to carry the melody, but not for long. Instead of another harmonica, he can now clearly hear the vibrations of a stringed instrument.

A violin instead of Knut's harmonica, and the sound is coming from...wait a minute...from the garden! Dale drops his harmonica. *My pitchfork, I need my pitchfork.*

With a rush of energy, Dale grabs his fork from the end of the row of potatoes and plunges it aggressively into the moist soil of the tulip bed. After a few thrusts, he exposes a caved-in wooden box, too decayed to offer any protection to the strings and mangy pieces of what once must have been a beautiful instrument.

As he looks up, he sees Knut's body grow grey and increasingly transparent. Knut reaches out and finally grasps Oda's hand. Dale tears his eyes from the couple and follows their gaze back to the garden.

Oda's cherished violin sheds its swollen, water-logged body and long-suffering strings like old skin. The reunited couple smile as the violin regains its glory.

How beautiful the well-varnished wood. How gracious the melody!

Dale stumbles backward to retrieve his dropped harmonica. He falls to his knees and grabs it. And he plays. He plays as if reborn, Knut's spirit guiding him, like a boy riding his first bike with a father's helping hand. The soft sound of the violin follows him and at times leads the way.

Dale can make out the fading young couple, but very faintly. He lets the harmonica fall to his lap. *It worked, it worked! They are together and happy!* Even though Dale can barely see them, their voices sound close and strong.

"At last," says Knut with a trembling voice, caressing Oda's silky hair. "When the fever took you, I lost heart. I lovingly buried your violin and left without looking back. It was too painful to stay."

"Oh Knut, I was there, but you could not see or hear me. I was the fog wishing to play my violin for you."

This is My Land

At last Dale has his answer to the strange, pervasive fog.

A thin white trail leaves, makes its way up, then disappears over the horizon. Dale places a loose fist on his chest. A sigh of relief comes out. He can feel the breeze lifting his hair as his eyes sweep the land below.

Dale picks up the precious violin and seems to float back to his porch. He turns around to look back at the garden, its vivid tulips, and the hole he dug.

I didn't dream the whole thing! The fog, the ghosts of the past, and the terrible sense that I don't belong are all gone.

He sits on his porch, the violin on his lap, smiling, a melody playing in his head.

Now, this is my land.

DIANE J. SOBER, a French Canadian native of the Quebec eastern townships, has been a successful Cape Breton transplant since 1974, taking in its rich culture. Her love of languages (German, Spanish, and some Mi'kmaq) coupled with her varied careers in mining exploration, fishing, oyster culture, and French Immersion teacher for the last 15 years, have been a source of inspiration. One could think that she did not want to wait for reincarnation to enter a new adventure each time. Presently working "out west" in Grande Prairie, Alberta, she plans to retire in her rustic River Denys home with her husband Stephen and be closer to their son Val in Inverness. Being a member of the Bras d'Or Stewardship Society, she fancies forever writing by its shores in her quiet moments, and biking to exhaustion when the desire hits her.

Teetering on the Edge

Voula Kappas-Dunn

Ethel Grant spotted a bald eagle close overhead. The orange of the bird's beak and talons punctuated its brown and white coloring.

"Did you see that?" she asked Morgan, her fourteen-year-old daughter, who had been dozing through the three-hour drive from Sydney to St. Margaret's Village.

"What? Where?" The girl sprang to life.

"An eagle! Your grandpa loved to track their movements. Grandma complained he wore binoculars around his neck the way other men wore ties."

When Michael Grant passed, family and friends thought it odd that he bequeathed his summer home to his only daughter while his wife survived. However, he had shared Ethel's interest in art, her need for peace and solitude and her brooding temperament.

Ten years after his death, Ethel pulled into the driveway of the remote cabin.

Despite fond memories of lazy summer days spent within its walls, she felt oddly unwelcome as she fiddled unsuccessfully with the lock. It was as if the house wanted to

Voula Kappas-Dunn

deny her entry. Her face burned red. *Could I have the wrong key?* All of a sudden, the door flew open.

Morgan, iPod in tow, scrambled out of the truck. She stared, ill-at-ease, at the unkempt garden and peeling paint, and then crossed the threshold of the small A-frame with trepidation, hesitant as a cornered fox.

"Mom, this place feels creepy. Look at the mess. I don't know why you want to live here."

"Making art is messy. It's perfect. You'll see."

Ethel unloaded her camera, laptop and art supplies. The slam of the truck door scared the birds out of the trees.

Ethel had decided to move into the old lodge on impulse, hot on the heels of her tenant's recent cancellation. Since her divorce, life had become unbearable, so the opportunity to escape town appeared heaven sent.

Morgan leaped across the main living space and out the back door where she took in the grounds which jutted out to the ocean. A short walk brought her to the edge of a cliff. Ethel watched her from the house, recalling a rope ladder that dropped to a rocky beach.

Morgan returned to explore the loft. "Mom, the view of the ocean is amazing. Can I sleep up here?"

Ethel agreed, giving the matter little thought.

As she entered the downstairs bedroom, she dropped her duffle bag, startled by the sound of a high-pitched, hard-to-discern voice. It seemed to whisper, *Why not end it here and now?*

This strange overture lasted no longer than a sneeze, and Ethel shook herself. *A trick of the mind, that's all.*

Unsteady, she climbed the stairs and half-heartedly attempted to fire up the wood stove before admitting that the task was beyond her. Instead, she turned to making ham and eggs in the galley kitchen. A loud bang caused her to jump. Feeling shot through with holes, like the sieve that hung next to the toaster, it took her a moment to realize that Guy, the neighbour, had knocked at the front door.

"Smells like breakfast," he said.

"Come in. Dinner. Not very fancy, I'm afraid."

🌡 Grey Area 🌡

Teetering on the Edge

They'd known each other as kids, though a five-year age difference separated them. Ethel trusted him with her spare key.

"I thought you might need help with the stove, to rid the place of the damp." Lean and tall, he looked awkward in the tiny entry hall. His sun-bleached hair set off muted blue eyes. The sturdy look of him caused her to smile. Like fine wine, he had improved with the passage of time, while she felt haggard, beaten down by her forty-two years.

"Good timing. I only just gave up on starting a fire."

He came in, circumventing a chandelier that hung in the entry. Ethel remembered it had once hung in her mother's front parlor. A 1980s castoff, it felt out of place with the rest of the décor of salvaged nautical finds. A glass-topped whalebone functioned as a coffee table, while a brass ship's porthole held a mirror, and strung-together shells acted as a curtain between the kitchen and sitting area. The seafaring touches belonged to her father. The place had been leased furnished and hardly altered by the seasonal tenants.

"The wood's damp," said Guy. "I stacked some drier pieces down below when I heard you were coming."

The basement stairs creaked as she followed him down. The cellar was as she recalled: a dank, stone labyrinth.

Back upstairs in moments, Guy quickly lit a fire showing her which vents to adjust and which ones to ignore. "Now when the wind's a-howling it changes the water in the beans, and you best do the reverse."

Ethel liked his language, as rich as the ocean once was when it teemed with cod, mackerel, crab and lobster.

As they walked outdoors to call Morgan for dinner they heard a scream.

"Mom! Help!"

The desperate voice sent them racing towards the cliff where Morgan hung from one side of the rope ladder, the supporting cable having split apart.

"I saw some rope downstairs!" yelled Guy.

"Hold on, honey! A line's coming!"

"Hurry," she cried back.

⚓ Grey Area ⚓

Voula Kappas-Dunn

Ethel crawled on her belly toward the cliff and held out her hand. "I can't reach you!" Moments later, eating dirt, she felt herself being dragged back from the rock face.

"You're going to get yourselves killed!" said Guy, as he wrapped a rope round a tree and threw her the end. "You need to hold it tight. There's no time for a knot!"

Frantic, Ethel stumbled over to the stunted spruce, its thick trunk firmly rooted despite exposure to sea and wind. While Guy let down the free end of the rope, she closed her eyes and prayed.

"Grab the line!" he yelled.

As Morgan obeyed, Guy pulled. Ethel opened her eyes and saw Morgan's hand come into view, followed by a crown of brown hair. Debris skittered noisily down the cliff face as she tried to get a foothold.

"That a girl!" said Guy.

Her daughter, the glue that held her life together, teetered, and then emerged over the grass-covered lip of the cliff. Guy grabbed her and pulled her up the rest of the way.

Morgan ran towards her mother.

Ethel, her limbs shaking with pent-up fear, embraced her daughter, tasting the salt that encrusted her skin, feeling its sting. She clung to the living, breathing wonder of her only child.

"Why didn't you take the long way?"

"I did. That's how I got down. On the way back, a voice dared me to climb the ladder. Mom, I know it sounds crazy, but it was as if the voice took over. I *had* to do it."

Morgan had always been a cautious child who abhorred sleepovers, avoided sports and over-studied for tests. Ethel's mind immediately went to her experience in the downstairs bedroom.

Guy listened without comment and Ethel had the feeling he was avoiding her eyes as he coiled the rope. *Could he be withholding something?* She tried vanquishing from her mind the sinister voice she heard earlier, but now it flooded her consciousness like tidewater.

&a Grey Area &a

Teetering on the Edge

One thing was certain. She wasn't going to sleep in the downstairs bedroom.

☙

Freshly bathed, Ethel lay next to her daughter in the king-sized bed that filled the loft. Before retiring, she had bandaged and applied lavender balm to their various bruises, brushed Morgan's hair to a gloss and let her own brown strands dry in a clip.

Empty teacups, stained with chamomile, lay on the nightstand while shadows filled the room. Out the window, fog obscured the view of the church and meadow down the shoreline. The repetitive sound of the foghorn acted like a soporific for Morgan and Ethel watched her fall fast asleep. Now that the surf no longer posed a threat, Ethel imagined it a lullaby. Even so, sleep eluded her.

☙

The next morning appeared clear and sunny. Ethel, still groggy, looked at a bottle of anti-depressants in her hand. The date of the prescription documented her discovery of Ross's ten-year-old extramarital affair, an event that had been broadcast in Frank Magazine, a local gossip rag.

His prominence as a builder with major commissions in Halifax, meant strangers discussed their break-up as if it were a fluctuation in the stock market, as if their marriage belonged to the public domain, and as if everyone held the right to voice an opinion or point a disparaging finger. She felt under constant watch, and kept even her closest friends at a distance.

She sought help from Dr. Snow, a psychiatrist, who became her sole confidant. "There are times when I think about ending it all," she confessed.

He raised an eyebrow. "How far have you thought this through?"

Voula Kappas-Dunn

"I Googled death by rope and ladder. It's considered painless and certain when done properly."

"And are these items in your possession?"

"In the tool shed, next to the Christmas tree."

"Sounds like a plan." The air conditioner hummed and the smell of coffee permeated his small office.

"There is a hook in my front hall closet. It measures eight feet from the floor, the minimum recommended height."

"Medication is in order. The stakes are too high. If you succeed, Morgan goes to Ross. I know you don't want that."

The meds kept her on an even keel despite the side effects for which she took two additional tablets. She pressed her tongue against their cool surface and swallowed. *Best to push the pain and rage away.*

Morgan entered the room, eager to head outdoors.

"How about helping me shoot some pictures?" Ethel spoke in a low timbre, attempting to summon her trademark winning way from before the gales turned on her.

"Sure. It's not like I have lots to do up here."

Neither discussed yesterday's near miss at the cliff, avoidance of all things unpleasant being the Grant family creed.

Raspberry bushes littered the roadside where they ventured. The gritty fruit tasted like tart jelly. Below, a bridge overlooked a gurgling brook that emptied into the ocean. Ethel preferred this little-known part of the Cabot Trail to the over-photographed Pleasant Bay featured in the Mazda car commercials. Rolling hills falling into the ocean sold well with tourists, but she felt ambivalent towards the subject matter.

Before she married, Ethel specialized in installation art, having enjoyed not one, but two acclaimed shows at The Power Plant, a Toronto venue for alternative art. The newlyweds returned to Sydney, the childhood hometown which ignored her work. Over time, she conformed to the needs of the local market, satisfying its appetite for pretty foliage and waterside views. All the while, her soul burned for meatier fare.

"Dad once spoke of building a house that overlooked the ocean," said Morgan.

Teetering on the Edge

Ethel hesitated. So many taboo subjects: her fragile mental health, Ross and his complicated situation and now the nagging feeling that the one place that afforded her privacy might be haunted. "Your father once dreamed of lots of things," she replied.

On the return journey, they descended into a cove. Ethel noted some kayakers setting up camp and spotted an eagle circling overhead. Beyond, a boy, about eleven, held out a fish at arm's length. The adults, off at a distance, seemed unaware of him but the presence of a favoured food source, dangling provocatively, did draw the eagle's attention. Morgan reacted immediately, racing toward the boy, out of Ethel's reach, oblivious to the danger to herself.

Ethel shook her head and looked around. She found and grabbed a sturdy branch and ran as hard as she could, the warm breeze striking her face, her heart beating fast.

The boy screamed, as the eagle screeched and dove for the fish.

"Help!" yelled Morgan, pounding over the sand.

What is she thinking? Unarmed, she too was fodder for the bird.

Ethel had almost caught up to Morgan when, for a moment, the eagle's huge wingspan obscured her view. The smell of fish filled her nostrils and panic gripped her gut. As if in the eye of a storm, she watched, dumbfounded.

The bird's talons raked the boy's face. The boy crumpled to the ground and the bird rose, blood glistening crimson against empty orange claws.

The fish landed at Morgan's feet. Still set on its prize, the girl in his way, the eagle thrashed its wings and pointed its talons in her direction.

Both hands on the stick, commanding all her might, Ethel swung at him, making contact.

It worked. Confused or perhaps injured, the eagle flashed a menacing look before he took to the sky. For some time afterward, Ethel heard the sound of his wings beating back the wind.

🐾 Grey Area 🐾

Voula Kappas-Dunn

Morgan escaped unscathed. Everyone on the beach headed towards the boy, who had sustained an ugly gash on the side of his face. His parents picked out bits of stone and feather from his cuts, and squirted water onto his face. Someone in the crowd proffered a first aid kit. While they waited for emergency personnel, Ethel obsessively checked the sky for the avatar's return—only half-listening to the thanks she received from the boy's parents.

She walked home distraught, her legs wobbling like someone who had been too long out at sea. "No matter what I do I can't keep you safe."

"I'm okay, Mom."

Ethel wanted to yell out, *I surrender!* Inexplicably, she felt the eagle somehow connected to the surreal events out on the cliff.

Back in the dubious comfort of the cabin, she wished for nothing more than the security afforded by four walls and a roof over their heads.

🐦

Her desire to view the proofs from the day's shoot, however, demanded confronting the downstairs bedroom. That gloomy space that possessed the only upgraded electrical outlet adequate for powering up her computer. Her fingers fumbled as she keyed in commands to alter lighting and crop the images. Mesmerized, she recalled halcyon days spent at art school.

Clinging to these memories lent her some buoyancy, yet she couldn't shake the feeling that the room elicited emotional pain—not hers, but someone else's.

Then, a presence stirred the air.

She fled into the hallway.

Get a grip. There's no-one there.

Refusing to give in, she re-entered the room and sat down at the computer.

🐦 Grey Area 🐦

Teetering on the Edge

"Are you doing all right?" she yelled out to Morgan, who was making lunch in the kitchen.

"Fine."

The smell of grilled cheese penetrated the makeshift studio. "I'm almost done," she yelled back. Her daughter's acknowledgement eased the tension in her neck and temples, allowing her to finish.

As she entered the kitchen, the phone rang.

Her mother's voice, raspy from years of smoking, said, "Remember to keep out of the woods. August means bear season. And tell Morgan 'no biking.' The dogs up north give chase to anything that moves. I hope you brought sun screen and loads of mosquito repellent."

Ethel listened, for once in her life inclined to take her mother's motto 'be prepared for everything,' seriously. She shuddered, recalling the chill of that...presence, only moments before. Then again, how was she supposed to prepare for what she could only describe, reluctantly, as the 'supernatural?'

"Mother, we're okay," Ethel lied.

During her marriage to Ross, she had become her mother: acting the part of the perfect wife married to the perfect husband, vigilant against outer danger, blind to inner discord. Could prolonged self-delusion lead to psychosis? And if so, where was the pill to make it go away?

By the time she hung up the phone and turned to face Morgan, she was all business. No need to share her growing alarm. *Better keep her close, though.*

When nightfall came, she tossed and turned again, dreaming of a hike she and Ross once made in nearby Ingonish. Breathing in the pine-scented forest, they napped on soft ground and walked along the sparkling coastline.

A loud scrape woke her.

The clock read three in the morning. She thought the sound came from outside. Careful not to rouse Morgan, she grabbed a flashlight, descended the stairwell, slid open the patio door, hesitated for a long while, and only then made her way to an overgrown rose arbor at the side of the house between her property and Guy's.

❦ Grey Area ❦

Voula Kappas-Dunn

Despite a lack of wind, a loose piece of fencing swung back and forth. She told herself to secure it and return inside, but some other impulse propelled her forward. She thought of Morgan on the rope ladder.

A sudden shift from grass to paving stones caused her to stumble and then trip on the gauze of her nightgown. She flung out a hand to brace herself and was startled when it came to rest on cold marble.

Dozens of roses filled the still air with their oppressive perfume. The flashlight wavered in her unsteady hand. The light passing over the stone illuminated the words

Lillian Stevens 1950-1980
Beloved Wife and Mother

Ethel dropped the flashlight and bolted for the house, a silent scream lodged in her throat.

Once inside, the room tilted and turned. Above her, the chandelier swayed. The hardwood seemed to heave causing her to slide and trip. Arms outstretched, trying to regain her balance, she looked up.

A pale figure, its neck encircled by a noose, stared with blue eyes inches from her face—dangling, grimacing. As she stared back, paralyzed, its head fell into her arms, weighted and clammy. Her fingers became entangled in dry, flaxen hair. She screamed. The head and the figure disappeared as the chandelier shuddered and lost its mooring.

Ethel stumbled backwards, but not far enough. The gaudy fixture plummeted, grazed her forehead, and crashed beside her. Glass shards exploded against the floorboards.

She looked down to see her arm slick with blood.

&

"Mother, wake up!"

Morgan's panicked voice.

Teetering on the Edge

Ethel opened her eyes and saw exposed wires on the ceiling. She couldn't tell how much time had elapsed. Everything felt unreal except for the pulsating pain in her head and arm.

While Morgan tended to her cuts, Ethel shared only that there had been a loose gate that awakened her before the chandelier fell.

Full recall slowly returned.

What of Lillian Stevens? What has she to do with me? Guy's mother, dead at age thirty, her name seldom mentioned. Ethel, of course, knew of the gravestone in the rose arbor, but last night, it and everything had taken on unreal qualities.

Ethel surveyed the wreckage: the light fixture—its chrome tentacles now bare of crystal ornament, the shards of glass reflecting pattern and color. Despite her state of mind and body, the arrangement drew her into a world of possibility. *With skilled lighting, the scene would make a striking photograph.*

Staring at the shards, Ethel envisioned disparate puzzle pieces clicking into place. *Everything must connect: tonight's horror, the near miss at the cliff, the eagle, the sinister presence in the downstairs bedroom.* But was she being handed a warning? Or being told a story?

"Let's deal with this mess in the morning," she said to Morgan. Her daughter was happy to agree.

Craving sleep, Ethel crawled back to bed.

᭰

The next day she jostled with her equipment, careful not to disturb the broken crystals. Cloud cover dictated the need for artificial lighting. She also brought up a ladder from the basement, the sound of rain plopping on the rooftop drowning out the creak in the stairs. Morgan checked all the rungs before allowing her mother to climb to the top.

"Crank up the radio," Ethel demanded, clicking the camera lens at breakneck speed.

᭰ Grey Area ᭰

Voula Kappas-Dunn

The Eagles' *Hotel California* came on. Immersed in her work, the lyrics stuck in her head well into the afternoon despite CBC Radio moving on to jazz.

The song was no accident. The dark undercurrents of success and addiction once held her and Ross captive, like the two partygoers in the '70s hit. Ethel's addictions were to spending, decorating her home, dressing in the latest style, and taking elaborate vacations, while Ross acquired sports cars, women and a taste for cocaine.

What of the eagle on the beach? Perplexed as to how everything fit together, she focused on something she understood—making art.

A plan for twelve oversized panels emerged. Drummer Don Henley's lyrics suggested titles for the images. "Pink Champagne on Ice," "Steely Knives" and "Such a Lovely Face."

As she worked, Ethel imagined Ross's paramour—her blond hair and silicone implants presented as objects of fascination, but dangerous like the wreckage at which she aimed her camera. Was the woman worth the little lies and betrayals Ross had fed her? Lies Ethel willingly, blindly, believed. She wished Ross had slept with his gay personal trainer instead. *Screwing the secretary was so clichéd.* Clearly, he lacked vision, but what did the whole fiasco say about her— the wife who never saw it coming?

Occasionally, she asked Morgan to position a light or black umbrella to counter the glare. All the while, Ethel snapped the shutter—she, a banshee on fire, lost in her inner dialogue, precariously perched on the ladder, crawling about the floor, contorted, feeling ghoulishly entranced.

The glass slivers glazing the floor spoke to her. She was in communion, but with what?

&

A seven-minute drive separated St. Margaret's Village from Bay St. Lawrence. The community hall, the location of that evening's annual crab supper, stood across the street from the

Teetering on the Edge

harbour and church, the same church Ethel glimpsed from her loft. The room smelled of cooked crustaceans and butter. Morgan headed towards a table of teenagers, leaving Ethel free to approach Guy.

"Good turn out," she said.

"It's the social event of the summer. Hottest ticket in town. Have a seat." He gestured to the empty spot across the table. "You're lucky to find one."

"Lately, I've been finding out all kinds of things," she said. "I guess you've heard about my divorce." Ethel wasn't sure why she brought it up—here and now. She so rarely talked to anyone about her personal life.

"I'm sorry," he said, sounding sincere. "You deserved better." He paused. "Is everything okay? Late last night, I noticed the lights on in your place. I thought I heard a crash."

She shook her head. There was no easy way to broach the subject. "I suspect I'm losing my mind." She picked up a crab leg, then pushed it to the side.

"How so?" The warmth of his smile encouraged her. She felt safe in his presence.

"I saw a ghost."

He blinked.

Ethel kneaded a piece of bread. "A noise woke me. I followed it to your mother's gravesite." She braced herself and looked directly at him. "I hate to pry, but what happened to her?"

He frowned. Despite the effort it cost him, his eyes met hers. "It's a hard tale to tell."

"Please, I'm hanging on by a thread."

He sighed. "My sister died in an accident and then my mother committed suicide. We found her suspended from a coat rack in the front hallway of your place. Afterwards, my father built the house I now live in and sold your father the old cabin."

"I'm so sorry. I had no idea."

"Never seen no ghost myself. Dad did, but then, he drank. Your father and the tenants after him never complained." Guy shrugged, and then asked, "Was it her?"

❧ Grey Area ❧

Voula Kappas-Dunn

Ethel nodded once, her eyes filling. They sat in silence for a moment and then she asked, "Could your mother be upset about something?"

"I recall her as gentle. An artist, like yourself. Self-taught. She loved to paint eagles. She was looking at the birds when my sister fell from the cliff. She couldn't forgive herself."

Ethel spine twitched. It all fit. But what did it have to do with her? She swallowed hard.

"The glass shards. I photographed them. The way they fell made for strong compositions. I'm certain it's my best work to date. I spent the afternoon printing the results." The clinking of silverware and the numerous conversations that had erupted around them made it difficult to continue. Ethel hadn't eaten a bite.

"How about we pack up that crab, find Morgan and head back to the house? I have an old light fixture I can install if you like.

"Thanks, I'd appreciate that."

"It's nothing. Besides, I'd like to see these photographs."

🐚

Morgan disappeared into the loft.

After retrieving Ethel's flashlight and replacing the broken fixture, Guy took an interest in one of the photographs she had taped to the wall. It resembled a multi-faceted gemstone.

She explained about the Eagles playing on the radio as she took the photos. "I'm calling that one 'Tiffany-twisted.'"

"Glad to hear you like the Eagles. I play their songs on the guitar. I do gigs here and there. You should come out and see me sometime."

At that, she offered him a glass of wine.

Am I playing with fire, inviting a man to a drink so soon after my divorce?

As they sat in the living room, the wood stove banged and the house groaned.

🐚 Grey Area 🐚

Teetering on the Edge

"Do you believe me that the place is haunted?" she asked, gathering her hair to one side.

Before forming a response, Guy stared at his wine. "People pick up energies, then interpret the situation in a way that makes sense to them."

"You mean they imagine things."

"That's not what I said. It's just that my mother wouldn't wish you harm."

"Something led Morgan to the rope ladder."

"All I know is that you seemed lost and vacant when you arrived, but now you look alive and vibrant. Whatever's latched onto you, it's brought life back into your eyes."

Curled up on the couch next to him, she breathed in his musky scent. Guy appeared to be taking in every curve of her slim figure, her best asset.

"You've got a gift for positive spin." She smiled. *Good God...I like him.*

Later, as she walked him to the door, he turned back. "Just one thing. No-one's ever installed satellite or cable. How did you pick up CBC Radio?"

"I don't know," she said, chilled.

After he left, she returned to the kitchen and switched on the radio. No matter where she flicked the dial, static filled the air.

She looked up at the newly installed light fixture and called out, "Lily! We need to talk."

🐚

The next day, Ethel performed a ritual she had picked up at a yoga retreat. She lit sage and smudged the rooms, inhaling the fragrant fumes in an attempt to rid herself and the house of negativity.

"We mean you no harm," she intoned. "Thank you for the photographs. Be at peace."

Feeling grounded for the first time since her arrival, she found a spot in the upstairs loft to meditate. It took twenty

Voula Kappas-Dunn

minutes of ruminating on her situation—where to send her photographs for processing, framing and eventual sale, how to entertain Morgan, and what to do about Lily—before she surrendered all thought. Her mind quiet, she sunk low into her being—trusting. An energy took up residence in her pelvis, and spoke to her.

I'm sorry I scared you. You were in turmoil. Morgan needs to take risks. Once, you could have shown her how, but you've forgotten.

"I remember now," Ethel said, aloud. Tears moistened her cheeks. When she opened her eyes she beheld a figure, filled with light. She knew the erratic Lily of the fallen shards, who had turned life in the remote fishing village upside down, would be at peace.

She whispered her father's name. At the time of his passing, Ethel, absorbed in raising a toddler, never fully mourned his passing. He supposedly died of a heart attack, but he had suffered from depression, and Ethel always suspected her mother had hidden the awful truth, one she dared not acknowledge.

Without words, the presence confirmed her fears: he'd taken his own life.

The experience felt familiar, an inexplicable state as ethereal as sunlight on water and infinitely sad. He and Lily had succumbed to the darkness, to the same inner abyss that had threatened to consume her. At this moment of realization, she also felt absolved of any guilt.

Afterwards, she rolled into a ball, mourning their loss, mourning Ross and the end of her marriage, emptying herself of tears.

&

As the summer progressed, Lily never returned. Ethel moved into the downstairs bedroom. She avoided mentioning the experience to her psychiatrist. She didn't need to. She had closure. She felt gratitude for her father, for their special relationship, for his intuition that she would one day need a place of her own—away from Ross. She felt the same appreciation for Lily.

Mother and daughter spent the summer snorkeling. The water's pristine clarity compensated for its frigidity, as did the spectacle of lobsters navigating the rocky bottom. Ethel showed Morgan how to take underwater pictures and the task absorbed them for hours. No longer preoccupied, Ethel delighted in her daughter's triumphs and accomplishments. In the evenings, Guy came by to serenade them. With his help, they replaced the old rope ladder, weeded the garden, and mowed the lawn, so that the beautifully situated A-frame oozed warmth and ease.

꒰ꔚ꒱

Two years later, Ethel flew to Toronto to attend the opening of *Eagle Eyes*, her long-awaited show. All twelve hand-colored prints sold to a single collector during the first hour, leaving her to chat with astounded newspaper columnists and fawning city dignitaries. She sparkled in a lamé mini-skirt, dazzling men half her age, while the women gushed over Guy, who played guitar.

The next day, Morgan read out the newspaper reviews.

"Mom, the art critics are calling you 'a visionary.'" Morgan offered her the stack of newspapers, but Ethel waved them away, smiling at her daughter.

"I can't believe you made all this happen, Mom."

"Neither can I," she answered.

Ethel recalled teetering on the northern edge of Cape Breton Island, her sanity and life in peril. She was thankful for the experience—all of it—right down to the scare of finding a ghost in her house.

The truth is, I didn't make it all happen. I had help all along the way. Unimaginable help.

꒰ꔚ꒱ Grey Area ꒰ꔚ꒱

Voula Kappas-Dunn

VOULA KAPPAS-DUNN received her Bachelor of Arts at York University in 1987 and currently lives in Sydney, Nova Scotia with her husband and two children. Two of her essays, on travel and shoes, are in the process of publication and will appear in an anthology entitled *Thirteen Ways From Sunday*. She is also working on a novel that takes place in fifteenth century Italy, Turkey and Greece.

Stillborn

Hugh R. MacDonald

The ball disappeared under the sun porch, rolling through an opening barely big enough for it to fit. Jack sighed loudly at his bad luck. Uncle Chuck had told him not to play with it in the first place, because it was autographed by his favourite player Dave Stieb, the first man to pitch a no-hitter in Blue Jays history. Jack thought he was being careful, just throwing it in the air and catching it in the glove, but the bright sun caused him to lose sight of the ball's descent.

Shielding his eyes, Jack knelt down and looked under the porch. He could see the outline of the ball in the darkness, but it was in too far to reach it with a stick. He'd have to crawl under to get it.

Jack loved visiting his grandparents for the long weekend in July every year, but he wished he hadn't been allowed to hear the ghost stories last night. His older sister, Janet, always told the scary stories—the true ones.

"Never go under Grandma's sun porch," Janet said, "because that's where she buried one of her babies. She thought it was dead—stillborn—but it could be heard crying for two days and nights. People say it's still there, waiting to get

Hugh R. MacDonald

someone young and fresh, waiting to steal their body and soul."

Janet had looked directly at him when she'd said those words: *steal their body and soul*. Jack didn't know how fresh he was, but he knew he was young. But now he had no choice. He had to get Uncle Chuck's ball. As he bent near the front steps, Jack said loudly, "It's not true. She just wanted to scare us kids."

Yeah, but she looked right at me. Jack's bravado was quickly quashed.

The sun shone through the latticework under the porch, generating varying-sized diamonds on the dark earth where the ball had come to rest. *At least there's a little light in there*, Jack thought.

The nails screeched as he pulled the wood aside. Sharp points reached for him and found their mark, as he squeezed through the small opening. He cried out as the nails pierced his back and drew blood. His mind on the pain, he scrambled forward. A few more feet and he would be able to reach it.

He breathed a sigh of relief, as his hand closed over the ball. Jack squinted to see if it had been damaged, and for the first time smelled the sour earth, as he inhaled deeply.

Janet's warning came flooding back. *Never go under Grandma's sun porch. Never go under Grandma's sun porch. Never go under Grandma's sun porch.* Panic overwhelmed him.

He pumped his legs in a backward motion, trying desperately to extricate himself from this dungeon, cursing himself for not heeding the warning, and for taking the ball in the first place. His foot dropped into a small hole and halted his retreat. Jack's heart beat liked a trapped bird's, as adrenaline raced through his body.

Afraid to look behind and nowhere to go ahead, Jack froze. The pause allowed him time to calm down. "Don't be silly. You're almost ten years old," Jack said loudly, his voice again resonating with a confidence he didn't feel. Pulling his foot free, he began to back up again, this time more slowly.

As he reached the small hole his foot had fallen into, Jack saw a sudden movement. *Probably just a mouse or a mole,*

Stillborn

he reasoned, but then he looked into the shoebox-sized hole, and saw something too big to be a mouse or mole, or even a rat.

A voice from his nightmares whispered, "Hi, Jackie. I'm Uncle No Name. Want to play ball with me?"

Jack watched tiny fingers reach from the opening. He felt them pull the ball from his hand. A body, no bigger than one of his sister's dolls, scurried from the opening. Milky eyes followed his, as he tried to look away.

"Stay with me, Jackie. Don't you want to stay with me?"

Jack's scream seemed to amuse the stillborn. The grin on its face displayed a perfect set of tiny teeth.

Babies don't have teeth, Jack thought, as the light went out of his eyes.

HUGH R. MACDONALD is primarily a writer of mainstream fiction, but loves to dabble in dark fiction as well. He has been published in print and online, and is the author of the YA novel, *Trapper Boy,* from Cape Breton University Press. Hugh resides in Cape Breton with his wife, Joanne and their cat, Beauty.

Grey Area

Katrina Nicholson

Somewhere in the distance, a dog barked.

It was the deep woof of a big dog, too persistent to sleep through. Paul Fosterling opened his eyes and found that all the colours were gone. Of the things he could see: a brick-sized rock right in front of his nose, the rain-soaked grass surrounding it, and the dense evergreen trees behind it, only the rock was the right colour. Everything else was rendered in shades of grey. He couldn't blame it on the darkness. It was night, but he could see everything clearly enough to know he was lying on his stomach in a forest in the rain.

How did he get there? The last time Paul had been in the woods, he was fourteen and being forced to play 'archeologist' with his six-year old cousin Ethan, whom he hadn't thought about in years. The game was Paul's brother Anthony's way of getting them to steal valuables from neighbours' houses.

Paul had always hated it, so he could safely assume he hadn't come to the woods out of nostalgia. Tequila was the more likely explanation. Paul was no stranger to waking up in odd places with gaps in his memory. It happened pretty much every time he went to one of Anthony's games and lost, but

Katrina Nicholson

he'd never known tequila to cause colourblindness. Maybe he'd tried something harder. Either way, he couldn't blame it on Anthony. Anthony had been dead for almost six months.

Paul pushed himself to his knees on arms clad in a blue plaid shirt. It was a moment before he realized that if everything else was grey, his shirt should have been, too. He looked down to see if the rest of him was in colour and saw a greyscale version of himself on the ground.

He must have tried acid to be tripping this badly.

He wore an unbuttoned blue plaid shirt with a ratty, navy blue t-shirt advertising a surfing company underneath, but the guy on the ground wore a hooded sweater. Paul and his colourless doppelganger had on the same too-long jeans with frayed bottom cuffs. They were held up with the same belt—the one he'd been poking extra holes in as he spent more money on games and less at the grocery store. The Paul on the ground had black skate shoes on his feet, but coloured Paul had only dirty white socks. Paul bent down and peered into his own face. His brown hair was now grey but still floppy and messy and in need of cutting. What little of his face he could see was covered in the same sticky black substance that was all over the rock.

The Paul on the ground was like a still-life portrait of a guy who'd hit his head on a rock. What Paul couldn't figure out was: how? Behind him loomed a densely forested hill too steep to climb. The steady *woof woof woof* of the unseen dog came from that direction. In front of him: more trees. Lots of them. And they were all grey, just like everything else except for his real body.

Out of the corner of his eye Paul spotted a white light in the distance. Turning away from the other Paul and the barking dog, he ducked under the low-hanging branches and headed toward the light. After a moment, he emerged onto a winding driveway with a beat-up old Ford pickup parked at the end. The light was the porch lamp of a rustic two-storey house set back into the woods. The rest of the house was dark and the drizzling rain made a faint grey halo around the naked bulb.

❧ Grey Area ❧

Grey Area

Paul walked up the gravel driveway in his socks. It should have hurt, but the LSD seemed to be dulling the pain the same way it had dulled his mind. He climbed the porch steps and looked through the window into the living room. Even though it was pitch dark inside, he could see the table lamp near the window, the fireplace, the sofa, and the rocking chair clearly. Paul could even feel electrons butting against the edge of the open switch inside the lamp, which was crazy. Even crazier, the lamp came on all by itself when Paul thought of it.

Paul shook his head, as if it could clear the drugs, and went to the door. Just as he raised his fist to knock, the door opened inward and a man stepped out. He was older, maybe mid-50s, with a puffy face and tired eyes like he'd just woken up. His grey hair, which was probably actually grey, was flat on one side. The man wore rubber boots and was pulling a rain jacket on over his pajamas. He reached back inside to pick up a flashlight from a table by the door and squinted at the metal barrel, feeling for the switch. Paul guessed he had left his glasses in the bedroom, because that squinty look was the same one Ethan used to get whenever they played together. Ethan's Nan had stopped letting him wear his glasses outside after he'd broken the third pair jumping off the roof of Mrs. Hoffsteader's garage.

"Call 9-1-1, just to be safe. I'll go and check it out," the pajama man called over his shoulder. Paul couldn't see who he was talking to, because everything beyond the doorway was now completely obscured by white mist, like a fog bank had just sprung up in their hallway.

Paul held up his hands, about to assure the pajama man that he wasn't a burglar, but the man didn't see him. He walked right through Paul. Jaw hanging open, Paul watched the man click on his flashlight and go down the steps as if nothing had happened. But something had happened. Paul Fosterling had just realized he was dead.

The selective colourblindness, the lack of pain, the fact that he wasn't wet or cold even though it was October and raining, the sticky substance on the rock, leaving the grey copy

Katrina Nicholson

of himself behind—they weren't symptoms of tequila abuse or a bad acid trip. They were symptoms of death.

He should be upset. Try to kid himself into thinking it wasn't true. Most people probably did. So, he tried.

Paul looked back over his life, trying to find something he regretted leaving behind, but there was nothing. Thanks to Anthony's 'friends' and their warehouse casino, he had no money, no real friends, no job, no apartment. Even his parents wanted nothing to do with him anymore. Compared to living, death didn't seem so bad.

Paul turned back to the house. He could see mist in the doorway, but not through the window. Weird. Maybe it was a clue as to where he was supposed to go now. Paul took a tentative step toward the fog. He was reluctant to go in without knowing what had happened to him, but what good was it to hang around in a place where people walked right through you?

Paul went to take a deep breath, realized he didn't breathe anymore, and stepped into the fog. It swirled around him, neither cold nor wet against his skin. In front of him there was nothing but more fog. Behind him... Paul glanced back. Behind him the pajama man had stopped moving. He was frozen in mid-stride near the first bend in the driveway.

A shuffling sound snapped Paul's attention back to the fog. A faint yellow light appeared ahead of him, bobbing slightly as it grew larger. Paul stepped toward it.

"Ah, ah," came a man's voice from the fog. "You wait right there and I'll come to you." The voice was faintly accented and quiet, like it belonged to an old man who had long ago been poor in London, but now lived in a library.

Paul obeyed. He watched as the yellow fuzz resolved into an old-fashioned lantern carried by an old-fashioned man. He was at least seventy, with a clean-shaven but wrinkly face and a shock of white hair streaked with grey. He wore a dark blue poorboy cap and a faded red neckerchief. His coat and trousers were made of dark, worn corduroy and his boots were scuffed and brown. In contrast to his ragged clothing, he held a shiny gold, pocket watch connected by a chain to a buttonhole in his ratty vest. He looked like he had walked out of a Charles Dickens novel.

Upon seeing Paul's face, the lantern man closed the watch and slipped it back into his pocket. "Best not to wander too far into the fog alone. Might get lost."

Paul opened his mouth to ask one of the million questions that had crowded into his head, but what came out was: "You're in colour."

The lantern man nodded. "Everything is, on our side."

"Why is it all black and white back there?"

"Because you don't belong there anymore."

"What about that man? He stopped moving." Paul pointed to the frozen, pajama-clad man, who was now only barely visible through the fog.

"Not stopped. Only slowed. Time moves much faster here."

As Paul stared at the man in the driveway, he noticed that the beam of his flashlight moved ever so slightly upward as his arm swung forward in extreme slow motion. "Where is 'here'?"

"Here is nowhere," the lantern bearer replied. "It exists only to be crossed."

"What's on the other side?"

The lantern man shrugged. "Whatever you've earned."

Paul swallowed nervously, an action that had no effect on his throat. He still didn't remember the past few hours, but he did remember the past few years, and he was worried what he had earned during that time wasn't good. "Do I have to go there?" Going back didn't seem like such a bad idea anymore.

The lantern man raised his light so it shone over Paul's shoulder. "Nothing left to go back to."

Paul looked and saw that the fog had closed behind him. Now there was nothing but white ahead and behind. The only clear air existed in the circle of the lantern's light. The lantern man turned and walked away, head down and shuffling. "This way."

Paul had no choice but to follow.

❧ Grey Area ❧

Katrina Nicholson

After a few minutes of walking, the fog started to get to Paul. He didn't like how it rolled in behind the lantern's light, closing them in. He scurried up alongside the lantern man to see if that would make it any better. It didn't.

To take his mind off imagining the terrible things that could be waiting up ahead for people who had only been to church two or three times in their entire lives, Paul tried to strike up a conversation.

"Who are you?"

The old man gave him a look that said the answer should have been obvious. "A crossing guard."

"No, I mean, what's your name?"

The old man's eyebrows shot up. Before answering, he hesitated for a second, like he barely remembered. "Tom. My name is Tom."

"I'm Paul," he said, offering his hand.

The old man had to transfer the lantern to the other hand to shake. When their hands touched, Paul felt it as a vague tingling sensation, like he'd interfered with an electrical current. He jerked his hand back, surprised, but Tom didn't seem bothered. In fact, the old man looked at Paul now as if he was a person rather than a job. It would have been a perfect time for Paul to bring up the subject of where they were going, but Paul chickened out. Instead, he asked about why he and his dead body were wearing different clothes.

Tom shrugged. "You appear how you see yourself."

Paul inspected his clothes and decided he must not have a very high opinion of himself. Tom smiled. "In time, you'll learn to change your form. It's a bit dodgy sometimes with all the little boys running around shaped like dinosaurs and whatnot, but you get used to it."

Before Paul could ask any more questions, the fog parted in front of them to reveal an enormous set of stone steps leading up to a columned building with a pointed roof. It looked like an old courthouse. It was grey, but grey like it was coloured grey, not like the colour had been leeched away. As eerie as the fog was, Paul had hoped the walk would be longer so he wouldn't have to face what was coming. As much as the building *looked* like it was made from pieces of carved stone, it felt like it had been created whole, complete with the laws governing its existence. It creeped him out that reality could be so fluid, and he didn't want to go in.

Paul followed Tom through the huge, polished wood door. He wasn't sure what he had been expecting on the other side—angels in flowing robes and halos, red demons with pitchforks, a glowing being dispensing judgement from a cloud, maybe. He definitely did not expect a cross between a modern airport and an old-timey train station, complete with the hustle and bustle. The floors were polished marble and the ceilings were high enough to fly kites, but the people walking to and fro were all just people. They wore more different styles of clothes than you would find in a costumer's warehouse, but they were definitely people.

He could tell right away who belonged here and who had just arrived. The staffers ignored the glittering paneled glass ceiling and the geographic murals carved into the walls as they went about their business, while the newbies crowded into long velvet-roped lines, trying to look everywhere at once. The lines filled most of the cavernous space, ending at a row of what looked like metal detectors. At the far end, set high on the wall, a massive screen, like the arrivals board at an airport, displayed information on people instead of flights.

Fosterling, Paul Henry. Born 18 March 1981, Gardiner, Massachusetts, USA

He found his name in the middle of the board between "Michner, Karlheinz Heinrich. Born 12 January 1933, Stuttgart, Baden-Württemberg, Germany," and "Botha, Tebogo. Born 30 August 1997, Lephepe, Kweneng, Botswana." As Paul read, his name moved down another place to make room for "Ming Ho, Kai. Born 7 October 2009, Xian, Shaanxi, China," at the top.

It seemed to Paul that the board wasn't so much written in English as capable of transferring information directly into his brain. He was too absorbed in trying to figure out how he could possibly have figured that out to notice Tom step aside to clear the doorway. Tom grabbed his shoulder, tugging him out of the way so a woman, wearing a brightly coloured, African tribal dress and carrying a torch, could lead a dark-skinned little boy in cut-off shorts into the building. The brief contact between Tom's hand and Paul's shoulder brought another tingling electric-current-like sensation. Paul jumped.

"What is that?" He asked, rubbing his shoulder.

A slim woman in a business suit and severely tied-back hair who Paul hadn't noticed before answered the question.

"You're a Spark now; made of energy. All interactions between us feel like that. You'll get used to it."

The woman, obviously some kind of clerk, dug around in the pile of paper on her clipboard as she spoke. She found the one she was looking for, clipped it to the front of the board, and looked up at Tom. "That will be all."

Tom turned to leave.

"Wait!" Paul protested, not wanting to lose his only ally so soon. He reached out to grab Tom's arm but stopped short when he remembered the electricity thing. "Can you hang around for a bit longer?"

Tom consulted his shiny watch and nodded. They followed the clerk as she marched briskly toward the lineups. Her heels echoed on the marble while she launched into a prepared spiel.

"Welcome to the Occluded Dimension. Here, Sparks like yourself who have shorn themselves of their physical bodies in the Matter Dimension can develop the ability to change form and to some extent the content of this dimension, depending on how much the now-useless laws of physics define your way of thinking. All Sparks are entitled to living space in the Final Destination Hotel and Casino, while tickets to Safe Harbor are awarded based upon merit. You can, of course, choose to pioneer your own colony, but you should know that most of these ventures fail, as true skill in manipulating latent energy into living space is extremely rare. Existing independent colonies can only be reached by

Grey Area

invitation. If you wish to settle in Safe Harbor, an immigration officer will consider your application momentarily."

At this, she stopped at the end of one of the lines and gestured for Paul to join it. He watched as a plump woman in a flowered dress stepped into one of the metal detector-looking things. Its attendant, a female officer in a subtle, navy blue uniform, watched the attached video screen as images flashed past.

"Your memories will be downloaded and screened by our immigration officers to determine your eligibility. Your chances of approval increase if you have someone from Safe Harbor to sponsor you." She gestured at two elevators set into the back wall, barely noticeable under the monstrous display. "News of your arrival has been broadcast to all the colonies. If someone is willing to meet you, he or she should be arriving shortly."

The modern, brushed steel doors of the elevator on the left had a scrolling LED panel above them. It read "Subway to Final Destination Hotel and Casino." Burgundy velvet ropes cordoned the elevator off from the rest of the hall. A burly man in a black suit and dark sunglasses guarded the entrance. The keypad on the door next to the elevator had only one button: down.

The elevator on the right had an old-style wooden pull-back grate in front of it. A weathered, wooden sign screwed to the wall at waist level read "This way to Safe Harbor Departure Lounge" in fading gold letters. Above it was an etching of an airship. A smiling old man in a uniform like a train conductor's stood by the button panel, which had only an up button.

An arrowed sign invited travellers going to "All other destinations" to proceed down the hallway to the right. As Paul watched, the right hand elevator dinged.

The clerk continued her spiel in a bored tone. "If you wish to appeal the immigration officer's decision or you want to apply for special dispensations such as re-anchoring in a new physical body or the work upgrade program, you can do so after you've been settled into your accommodations."

Katrina Nicholson

The attendant slid the grate back and tipped his hat at the elevator's occupant—Paul's Nan. Well, she wasn't actually related to him. She was Ethan's grandmother on his father's side. She'd told Paul and Anthony to call her Nan whenever they visited so they wouldn't confuse Ethan, who was only three when he went to live with her. Behind her back, Paul and Anthony had called her 'Old Hag.' Not because she was mean, but because Anthony was. Paul felt ashamed of it now. Given how he and Anthony had turned out, Paul considered it lucky that his family had moved away to Chicago when they did. It probably saved Ethan from turning into a little shit with a juvie record.

Nan looked exactly as he remembered, even though he hadn't seen her since he was fourteen: mid-sixties, in a pastel pink cardigan and long skirt. She wore the same chunky shoes and had the same tightly-curled style to her short, grey hair. Paul hadn't kept in touch with her or Ethan after his family moved away. He hadn't even known Nan died. He wondered how it happened, but it seemed rude to ask.

Despite the fourteen year age difference, Nan recognized him right away. She rushed over, arms open, and enfolded him in a hug. "Oh Paul, it's so good to see you again." She held him at arm's length and scrutinized his appearance. "Do you really see yourself like this, honey? The twenties are a bit young. And those clothes..."

Paul's embarrassment didn't flush his cheeks, because he didn't have blood anymore, but it was written all over his face just the same. "Uh, Nan, I *am* in my twenties...or I was. And I dress like this all the time."

Nan clapped her hand over her mouth in horror. "Oh gracious, I thought more time had gone by! Dead in your twenties! What happened?"

Paul wondered the same thing, but he was no closer to an answer now than he had been when he woke up atop his own dead body. All he had was a curious sense that it had something to do with Ethan. After fourteen years of barely sparing a thought for his cousin, everything seemed to remind him of the kid today. "I'm not sure," Paul answered. "I don't remember leaving Chicago, but I woke up in the woods—"

Paul's explanation was interrupted by a commotion from the front of the line. Two bouncer-types in dark sunglasses grabbed a robed guy in his mid-thirties who had long brown hair and a goatee. He would've looked like Jesus, except he was dragging his feet and screaming at the top of his lungs.

"No! God told me to do it! I demand to talk to God!"

"Sir, I assure you that the being you refer to does not exist. This plane is administered by the Counsel of the Occluded Dimension," responded one of the bouncers as they hauled the Jesus guy toward the steel elevator.

"COD," Nan whispered to Paul. "It confuses a lot of people."

"Furthermore," said the other bouncer, "they have neither the authority nor the ability to interfere with the matter dimension."

Something about the twisted expression on the Jesus guy's face twigged Paul's memory. He tried to imagine the guy with shorter hair and no beard. "That guy looks familiar," he told Nan.

The clerk dug through her papers. "His name is Nelson Francis Wilmont. Born the 21st of April, 1975 in Decatur, Illinois, USA."

"Wait, Nelson Wilmont? The Garbage Bag Strangler?" Wilmont had snatched four women from L-train stations, choked them to death with ropes made of braided garbage bags and dumped their bodies in Lincoln Park. The Chicago police had plastered security camera stills of Wilmont's sneering face everywhere during the manhunt.

"He was killed in a police shootout late last night," the clerk told him. "Obviously, he was denied entry to Safe Harbor. People such as Wilmont, who pose a danger to others, are deported to the Final Destination Hotel."

Paul watched the bouncers stuff the struggling serial murderer into the steel elevator with the help of their identical triplet, who had been guarding the door. It made him realize two things. One: the bouncer wasn't there to keep people out, but to keep them in, and two: if the immigration officer ruled against him he'd be stuck down there with people like Nelson Wilmont, who saw themselves as Jesus and strangled people for fun. He knew for certain he wasn't creative enough to build his own colony from nothing.

"What...what will happen to him down there?" Paul managed to ask as the elevator dinged again and the doors closed, shutting Wilmont inside with the two bouncers.

"I have no idea," the clerk told him breezily. "The Council doesn't meddle in their affairs as long as they stay down there out of everyone else's way. However, since our lack of physical bodies makes it impossible for us to feel pain anymore, the most they can really do is to annoy each other."

Almost as soon as the doors had fully closed they dinged again and re-opened. As they slid apart, they revealed not Wilmont and the bouncers, but Anthony. He looked 29, the same age he'd been when he died, but instead of the cheap, grey suit their parents had buried him in after he was shot to death in a fit of anger by one of his marks, he wore an expensive, jet black, custom-tailored three-piecer with matching gleaming Italian shoes. With his skinny frame, slicked-back black hair and pale skin, Anthony should have looked like a wealthy undertaker, but his getup screamed "Organized Crime." He strolled off the elevator like he owned the place, adjusting his gold cuff-links and nodding a condescending greeting to the bouncer.

The clerk's mouth flattened into a disapproving line that mirrored Nan's expression.

"Regrettably, representatives from the hotel are permitted to make their case to the immigration officers when they have an interest in the applicant in question," the clerk told Paul. She had been moderately helpful before, but now she was cold, obviously suspecting the worst of him now that she knew he was connected to someone like Anthony.

Nan glared at Anthony as he approached. "I should have known that rotten apple would show up for this. Don't you worry, though, Paul. You were always a good boy. You'll be

Grey Area

coming with me to Safe Harbor. You'll love it there. I've been telling Miriam and Benjamin all about how wonderful you were with Ethan when you were kids and they're looking forward to meeting you."

Paul's Aunt Miriam was Ethan's mother. She and Uncle Benjamin had been killed when their Land Cruiser ran over an anti-tank mine on the way to an archaeological dig in Cambodia. Ethan had talked nonstop about their adventures when he was a kid and Paul had always regretted that he'd never gotten to meet them.

"My condolences to our aunt and uncle then, Nan, because Paul won't be joining you in the land of boredom and apple pie. He'll be coming with me," Anthony said as he joined them. He winked at Paul. "People like you and me need more stimulation, right Paulie? You'll love it down there. Money, girls, poker games that never end—"

Paul clenched his fists so he wouldn't punch his older brother in the face. "Don't talk to me like we're the same, you son of a bitch. I know what you did. They paid you to sucker in people like me. Get us hooked."

Anthony grinned. "Yeah Paulie, and I know what you did, too. I know where all that money you were losing came from."

Paul looked at the floor, burning not just with anger, but with shame. He'd alienated every friend he had by begging, weaseling, and conning them out of their money. He'd even stolen from his own mother. When he died he'd been at the end of his rope. Anthony's 'friends' had made sure he always had a spot at their poker tables so he would slide deeper and deeper into their debt. He'd been willing to do anything to get more money. Anything. Even after he'd found out the truth about their 'casino' he still couldn't stop himself from going back.

Whatever happened that had led to him being dead in the woods was surely the result of some desperate scheme to get cash. Not so he could keep Anthony's buddies from breaking his legs, but so he could play it at the tables and turn it into more. Even though it never, ever, turned into more for

Katrina Nicholson

longer than a few minutes, he always held out hope, because he was addicted. And it had all started with Anthony.

Nan looked from Anthony's smiling face to Paul's angry one. "Anthony, do you know something I don't?"

Anthony's predatory smile widened. "Probably. You haven't seen him in a while. I on the other hand..."

"Never mind. I'll find out during the scan," Nan said. She took Paul's arm, producing another tingling sensation, and led him into the lineup for the scanners. "Don't worry, sweetheart," she told Paul as he fumed. "Whatever it is I'm sure we can explain it to the immigration officer. They're not bad people you know."

Paul loved her for believing in him, but deep down he knew what the officer's decision would be and that he deserved it. He could have gotten help. His parents had offered to pay for counselling and rehab many times, but he'd always refused. The worst part was that as much as he wanted to go with Nan, to meet Ethan's parents, there was a part of him that had had been drawn to the steel elevator ever since he'd seen the word 'casino' above it.

Nan gave Paul a reassuring pat on the shoulder and went up the aisle between the lines with Anthony. They approached a counter labelled 'Sponsors: Check in Here' and they leaned over to talk to the officer sitting behind it. Paul couldn't hear what they were saying, so his eyes strayed to the scanners and the screen which would soon be displaying the sordid highlights of his life.

The line slowly shrank in front of him, until finally no one stood between him and the scanner. An immigration officer waved him forward, and Paul, feeling trapped by the inevitability of his banishment to an eternity of compulsive card playing, friendlessness and debt, backed away. Paul gestured for the dark-skinned little boy in shorts to go ahead of him.

"The scan is necessary to process your application," the clerk explained impatiently. "If it doesn't go your way you can appeal or apply for work placement once you get down there..."

🍃 Grey Area 🍃

Grey Area

Paul shook his head. How could he explain to her that once he got down there he would never want to leave? "No. I don't want...I can..."

The clerk rolled her eyes. "Fine. If you want to be that way, I'll just have to get Barry to give you a little push. You're holding up the line."

She strode away, leaving Paul alone with Tom, whom Paul had forgotten was still there. The two of them stood aside as a steady flow of people moved past them into the scanners.

"Easy now," Tom soothed. "She's right. Everyone who wants in badly enough to work for it gets there eventually. And if you're worried about controlling yourself, ask one of those muscular fellows to stay with you until your work placement papers go through. How's that sound?"

Paul was immensely relieved by Tom's suggestion. It was enough to stop the screaming panic-monkey ravaging his thought processes. He slid down the wall and sat on the floor, resigned. Tom set his lantern down and took a seat next to him.

"That's what you're doing, isn't it? Work upgrade?" Paul asked.

Tom nodded, fiddling with his gold pocket watch. "That's what we're all doing. Me, that lady clerk, the immigration officers, those bouncers by the elevators. We've got to show we mean it."

Paul looked at the viewing screen. "I just hope when they see it, they won't hate me."

Tom shrugged. "Everyone's done things they're not proud of."

"I know, but I've done some things...a lot of little things, actually, and I can't shake the feeling that there's something bigger, but..." Paul shook his head. "I just can't remember."

"It'll come back in time," Tom assured him.

At that moment, the gold pocket watch emitted a beeping sound like a digital alarm clock. Tom opened the watch. It revealed a circular display containing similar information to what was on the board at the end of the hall—name, date and location. But while the arrivals board showed

Katrina Nicholson

birth dates and locations, the watch showed the date and location of death. It also included a picture of the deceased, presumably so Tom could recognize them when he went out to guide them through the fog.

"Sorry," Tom began, "I've got to go..." He trailed off when he saw Paul's face and the way he was staring in horror at the watch. It read:

Hackett, Ethan Benjamin. Died 03:59 EST, October 19th, 2009, East Stone Arabia, New York, USA

Ethan's picture brought everything back. In it, Ethan was twenty years old, his hair unruly and unclassifiably-coloured, somewhere between red, brown, and blond. His muddy green eyes shone with mischief and intelligence and he smiled in the same crooked, guileless way as he had yesterday afternoon when he opened the door of his Boston dorm room to find Paul standing on the step. They hadn't seen each other in years and Paul looked like a homeless person, but Ethan had let him in, no questions asked. Even the dog hadn't blinked.

Ethan hadn't asked why Paul needed the money. He'd just gone to the bank and withdrawn it. The money had been set aside for Ethan's schooling after his parents died. More than anything else in the world Ethan wanted to follow in their footsteps and be an archeologist, but he'd given his tuition money to Paul anyway. Just like when they were kids, Ethan would do anything for his cousins. And Paul had let him. He had also let Ethan blow off a midterm to drive him home. For that alone Paul deserved a one way elevator ride downward. But it got worse.

The tequila, for example. Paul hadn't told Ethan he'd been sneaking sips of it out of a flask for hours when, in the middle of Nowheresville, New York, a little after three in the morning, Ethan had asked him to take a turn at the wheel.

Paul had managed to keep Ethan's labouring old diesel Golf on the road for almost an hour before the deer jumped out in front of them. A jerk of the wheel, a looming tree, crunching, some breaking glass, and a sleeping Ethan compressed between his seat and the dashboard were all Paul took in before he was thrown from the car and down the steep embankment because (naturally) he wasn't wearing his seatbelt.

One minute the kid had goals, a plan, a future, the next: nothing. The only part of his parents' footsteps he'd managed to follow was the part where they died senselessly before their time.

It was Paul's fault, and he couldn't stand it. "How long?" He managed to ask.

"It just came in. Less than a second, their time."

Paul shot to his feet, surprising Tom. "I have to help him." He shouldered his way through the lines toward the door.

Tom scrambled to gather up his watch and lantern before chasing after him. "You can't go back. Sparks are supposed to leave the Matter Dimension to those still anchored in physical bodies. That's why the fog is there. Only the crossing guards are given lights that can make a path."

Paul turned and tried to snatch the lantern from Tom's grasp, but the old man had a grip like iron.

"Do you know how many people try that? You can't take it. That's how it was designed."

"Then lead me or let me get lost in the fog, because I don't care if I get in trouble or not. I'm going back."

Paul charged through the foyer, barreling right into the clerk and Barry, who turned out to be one of the bouncers.

"That's him!" the clerk exclaimed.

Barry clamped down on Paul's shoulders. His grip was no mild tingling but a full-on electric shock. It didn't hurt, exactly, but it was immobilizing. Paul felt his knees giving out.

"Paul! Think smaller!" Tom shouted from behind him.

It sounded like absurd advice for dealing with a 350 lb. muscle-bound bouncer with a grip like a vice, but only according to the physical laws he was used to. Here, Paul remembered, he could change things if he wanted to. And he really, *really*, wanted to.

Paul groped around in his memory for something smaller and latched onto the first thing he thought of.

Katrina Nicholson

Barry's surprise at finding himself suddenly gripping the empty space over the head of a yellow Labrador Retriever manifested as a brief flickering of his form, from bull-necked bouncer to scrawny, nerdy teen, and back again.

"What? He's not supposed to be able to do that yet! He just got here!" Barry exclaimed.

"Come on!" Tom yelled, waving at dog-Paul from the heavy door at the end of the hall.

"Why are you helping him?" screamed the clerk. "Barry, stop the dog-man!"

Dog-Paul shot under the bouncer's legs and in the second it took for Barry to change form from lumbering human to sleek cheetah, Paul made it to the door. Tom slammed it shut behind him.

Barry the bouncer's cheetah paws skidded on the smooth marble as he tried to stop himself from crashing into the door, but he was going too fast, so he settled for shifting into a marshmallow to soften the impact. He was back to human and on his feet in a split second. He opened the door just as the clerk ran up to join him but they were too late.

"Damn," Barry said.

The clerk brushed it off. "Oh well. He'll just become one of those anchorless losers drifting around in a world they don't belong to anymore. When he eventually comes back here—and he will—this and anything else he does while he's over there will be on his record."

Barry shrugged. "Maybe it'll be better than what he's got on there now."

🐾

"Where did you get the form?" Tom asked, holding the lantern high as he and dog-Paul ran together through the fog.

"It's my cousin's dog, Brody," Paul answered. As he let go of the dog's image in his head, he felt himself spring back to his original hobo-esque form like a stretched rubber band.

A fuzzy outline of the dark, rainy dimension they'd left behind appeared ahead of them in greyscale. The man in the

🐾 Grey Area 🐾

pajamas who had been frozen in the driveway had only moved two steps while they'd been gone. As Paul and Tom burst out of the fog onto the porch, the man unfroze and began briskly walking down the driveway, picking out a path ahead of his feet with the flashlight beam.

Paul ignored the driveway and ran into the woods. "This way. It's faster!"

Tom and Paul cut through the trees, heedless of the dense, pointy branches they passed right through. Soon they reached the bottom of the embankment where Paul's body lay. As they ran, the dog's barking got louder.

"Up here," Paul said, charging up the steep incline toward the road he now knew lay at the top. It was fifty feet up at an angle of more than 45 degrees, but Paul and Tom didn't stumble or slide in the mud. Paul watched his sock pass through a mound of dirt that should have tripped him up.

"How am I doing that?" Paul asked. "If I can pass through that, why don't I just fall right through the earth?"

"You're used to gravity," Tom replied, not panting, because there was no physical component to their exertion. "You're automatically using the Earth's magnetic field to keep you on the surface."

Shoving aside all the possibilities *that* little fact opened up, Paul leaped over the crest of the embankment onto a two-lane county road in the middle of nowhere. Despite the darkness, Paul could see the misting rain collecting into reflective puddles and several black, viscous drops of deer blood on the road ahead. Paul did not see the deer, but ten feet farther on, he saw Ethan's old Golf, a rusty orange in real life, but grey to Paul's eyes now. The car was wrapped around a tree on the right hand side of the road. Brody stood beside the car, pawing at the passenger door and woofing his call for help. When he saw Paul, he ran over, barking frantically, his golden eyes wild,.

Paul looked at Tom in surprise. "He can see us?"

Tom shrugged. "Animals can't learn science. Their minds are a lot more open to this sort of thing."

Katrina Nicholson

Paul let Brody lead him to the car. Ethan sat in the passenger's seat, still buckled in, his chest compressed by the misshapen dashboard. Small cuts on his face leaked blood from the broken windshield, but otherwise his body looked intact. Most worrisome was the fact that Ethan's skin was turning from grey to pink.

"He's starting to come out! How long has it been?" Tom checked his pocket watch. "27 seconds."

"There's still time," Paul insisted, turning to Ethan. He tried to grab the passenger door handle, but his hand passed right through both the mangled car door and his cousin's body.

"Dammit! How do I get him out?"

"You can't interact with matter anymore, but I have heard of some anchorless Sparks developing the ability to generate electric and magnetic fields," Tom replied. "The door handle is metal. Try exerting yourself on it."

Paul didn't need any help building up power to use against the offending door handle. He was freaking out. As he turned his focus onto it, he understood how its molecules were latticed together and how they could be made to move. With a squeal of twisting metal the entire passenger door ripped free of its mountings, forcing Brody to leap out of the way. The door hurtled through Paul and Tom's incorporeal forms before skittering a hundred feet down the highway in a shower of sparks.

Tom was astounded. "Quite the fast learning curve you've got there."

But Paul wasn't listening. He stared in agony at Ethan. The kid's eyes were closed and his face peaceful, like he'd fallen asleep. Only the blood gave it away. Brody stood on his hind paws and licked Ethan's face. Paul performed a less forceful version of the yanking manoeuver on the seat mountings. He used them to lift Ethan, seat and all, out of the car and tip him onto the ground as gently as he could manage.

As Ethan's body slid onto the wet roadway, Paul noticed that even though Ethan had been wearing jeans and a t-shirt a minute ago, he now had on tan cargo pants and an army green

🐾 Grey Area 🐾

Grey Area

sweater. Paul started in surprise as Ethan's eyes opened and fixed on Paul. They were brownish green and confused. They darted from Brody, who was hovering anxiously near his master, to Paul.

"Paul?" Ethan asked as he tried to sit up.

"Lie back down!" Paul ordered.

Ethan hastily obeyed, his energy form phasing back into his matter one. "Why? What's going on?"

Paul looked at Tom, who was standing in the roadway holding the lantern and watching them.

"What are you going to do?" Tom asked.

"Who are you?" Ethan asked, as he noticed Tom.

Paul's hands tingled as he rubbed them together. He was thinking of the lamp in the pajama man's house and how he'd been able to turn it on from outside just by thinking about what the electrons wanted. He needed to make that happen again.

Paul hurriedly turned back to the car, feeling around under the hood with his new electric sense. He found the trapped electrons he knew belonged to the battery and pulled. The battery tore free of the mangled hood and set down inside Paul. He knelt next to Ethan's chest, feeling the electrons looking for a way out of the battery and finding his body. They flowed into him, boosting his natural energy levels.

"Brody! Back!" Paul shouted. The dog dashed off the shoulder onto the gravel, dancing his anxiety as Paul raised his hands over Ethan.

Ethan stared at the battery. "What's that? What are you—"

Ethan's question turned into an agonized scream as Paul spanned his hands across the kid's chest on opposite sides of his heart and let loose the electrons that had built up inside him. Ethan's body arched, his back completely leaving the pavement, and when it hit the ground again, Ethan's colour was gone.

Paul slumped back on his butt in relief as Ethan lay panting on the road, eyes squeezed shut and hands twisted up in his t-shirt. Tom stepped to Paul's side and showed him the face of the gold watch. It was blank. No more entry for Ethan.

"That was extraordinary. Most of the anchorless Sparks I've seen take tens, sometimes hundreds of years to master making electric lights flicker or swinging a door closed by its hinges."

"Don't call Guinness just yet," Paul said ruefully. "I think most of it was adrenaline."

Tom raised his eyebrows at that. "You haven't got adrenaline anymore."

Tom was right. Paul didn't have adrenaline, or even a circulatory system that could have carried it, but he did have its effects. He looked at his hands, feeling like they should be shaking, but they were steady.

Brody started barking again a split second before a flashlight beam pierced Tom's body. The pajama man finally reached the end of his winding driveway and made his way down the road toward them.

"Hi there," the pajama man called out. "What's all this noise about?"

Paul darted a glance at Tom. "Can he see us?"

Tom had frozen in the beam, which continued through him and lit up Brody, who was still standing at the side of the road. "He shouldn't be able to—" Tom began. Before he could finish, the flashlight beam slid off Tom and found Ethan lying on the road.

"Jesus!" the pajama man exclaimed, jogging up the shoulder toward the kid, who still had his eyes closed and was clutching his chest. "Hang on, son. The paramedics are on their way."

As if summoned by the pajama man's assurance, Paul heard sirens in the distance. The pajama man turned around, shouting and waving his flashlight to flag down the ambulance as it came around the bend. Brody ran to the man's side and added his barking to the mix. The ambulance screeched to a halt in front of them, splashing puddle water onto Brody and the pajama man. As Brody shook it off, two uniformed EMTs— one a gruff older man and the other a skinny boy barely out of

Grey Area

high school—jumped out and rushed to Ethan's side with their kits. Paul and Tom stood very still as the paramedics looked Ethan over.

"He's still breathing," said the younger one.

"Can you tell us where it hurts?" asked the other.

"My...my chest..." Ethan wheezed.

"Keep the dog back," the older paramedic ordered as Brody's nose jutted into his personal space.

The pajama man grabbed Brody's collar and flattened his other hand on Brody's behind, encouraging him to sit and be still.

Brody vibrated with impatience as the younger paramedic gently pried Ethan's hands off the t-shirt while the older one whipped out a pair of scissors and deftly cut it off. Paul, Tom, the pajama man, and both paramedics gasped when they saw what it had been hiding.

"Holy crap," the young paramedic exclaimed.

Burned into the skin on either side of Ethan's heart were two perfectly defined hand prints.

"What the hell did that?" the younger guy squeaked.

"Well clearly his hands must've been between the dash and his body when the..." The older paramedic floundered as he inspected Ethan's uninjured hands. "Listen, forget about that. Dress the burns, will ya?"

"Is there anyone else here? Were you the only one in the car?" the younger paramedic asked Ethan as he began to bandage the kid's chest.

"No...my cousin..."

The older paramedic looked Ethan in the face. "I need you to open your eyes for me, okay bud? I need to know your cousin's name and where you think he went."

Ethan's eyes fluttered open, squinting as he tried to focus on the paramedic's craggy face.

"Not wearing your glasses, as usual," Paul chuckled.

Ethan's eyes slid away from the older paramedic and met Paul's dead on. "His name is Paul," he said. "And he's sitting right there."

☙ Grey Area ☙

Katrina Nicholson

The older paramedic followed Ethan's gaze. "I don't see anyone."

Paul stared back at Ethan, shocked. The colour had gone from the kid's body but the green remained in his eyes. "Ethan...can you see me?"

"Of course I can see you. And I can hear you too. You're right there with that old guy," Ethan replied irritably. "He's right *there*," Ethan insisted to the paramedics, lifting his arm to point.

The paramedics looked at each other. "Hallucinations," the older decided.

Paul turned to Tom. "How can he see us? I thought it worked!"

"It did," Tom replied. "You re-anchored his Spark in that body. I guess it just remembered how to see. I've heard of it happening."

"Ethan, listen," Paul said urgently, "They think you're crazy. Just tell them you saw the light reflecting off the rain or something."

"But..."

"No, Ethan, shut up. Tell them my body is down there in the ravine."

"How...?"

"Because I'm dead, Ethan."

"You can't be dead."

The paramedics stopped shining penlights in Ethan's eyes. "Who can't be dead?" asked the younger one.

"My cousin," Ethan explained, looking away. "I thought I saw him there, but it was only a trick of the light. I'm pretty sure he's dead. He flew out of the car down that way," Ethan pointed in the direction Paul indicated.

Brody broke free of the pajama man's grasp and led the younger paramedic over the embankment while the pajama man helped the older paramedic strap Ethan to a stretcher. Tom and Paul stood off to the side, out of the way. Paul kept one eye on the fog, which hovered in the open doorway to the back of the ambulance.

🐚 Grey Area 🐚

Grey Area

"What does it mean, that the fog followed me?" Paul asked.

"The fog doesn't exist in any one place. You get to the Occluded Dimension by making a sort of mental side step. Your mind must be equating that possibility with doorways to make it easier to understand." Tom hesitated before adding: "Will you come back and straighten things out with the council now that your cousin is safe?"

Brody and the young paramedic returned from the ravine. The older guy gave him a questioning glance and he shook his head sadly. Brody hung his head. Paul watched Ethan's confused expression as the paramedics gave him the news.

"I can't go now and leave Ethan broke, half dead and seeing ghosts. I mean, if he's not careful—and that word isn't in this kid's vocabulary, trust me—they'll have him locked up in a rubber room before you can say 'schizophrenic.' I have to stay and help him."

"What should I tell the Council?" Tom asked.

"Tell them I made a mess of the kid's life and I'd appreciate it if they gave me a chance to sort it out. Then I'll go back and work for the rest of forever in the placement program. I promise."

Tom nodded and faded out as he merged with the mist.

Brody leaped into the fog hovering in the doorway to join Ethan inside the ambulance. Paul slipped past the pajama man and through the side to avoid the fog. He sat on the bench next to Ethan's stretcher as the two paramedics spoke to the police, who had just arrived to secure the scene.

Paul and Ethan looked at each other, then looked away, unsure of what to say. Brody tried to lean against Paul's leg and stumbled when he passed right through. Paul and Ethan both laughed at the dog's confusion. Before Paul could say anything, the paramedics returned.

"The dog can't come in the ambulance," the older paramedic said, trying to drag Brody out by his collar.

Katrina Nicholson

Brody, normally the world's friendliest dog, bared his teeth and growled at the paramedic. Ethan laid a reassuring hand on the dog's head.

"He can unless you want to leave me out on the road too," Ethan said stubbornly.

The younger paramedic asked, "Can't you leave him with that guy?"

"No."

The paramedics exchanged a glance. The one who would be riding with Ethan shrugged.

"Whatever," the older one grumbled. "Suit yourself. If he bites you, don't blame me." He shut his younger colleague in the back of the ambulance with Ethan and the dog.

The young man busied himself getting ready for the drive to the hospital.

"I'm sorry about all this," Paul said.

Ethan shrugged. "It's no big deal. I'll be fine."

Paul shook his head. The kid was unflappable, as always, but far from fine. The young paramedic shot Ethan a worried glance as he seemingly stared at—and talked to—thin air. At that moment, Tom returned, surprising everyone but the paramedic.

"It's all settled," Tom told Paul, crowding into the ambulance and ending up with his legs occupying the same space as Paul's right arm and his head half inside a cabinet full of medical supplies.

"What's settled?" Ethan asked.

Paul shushed the kid as the paramedic gave Ethan another odd look.

"You were right. He does need help," Tom said, looking at Ethan. "Which is why the Council agreed with me that he should be your placement in the work program."

"I can do that? Here?" Paul asked, holding up a hand to forestall more questions from Ethan.

"It's not usually permitted, more because interacting with this dimension is difficult to impossible for most Sparks, but good is good, regardless of where it's done."

⚜ Grey Area ⚜

Grey Area

Paul stared at Tom, unable to properly express his gratitude. Tom had really gone above and beyond anything Paul had any right to expect, and he couldn't figure out why.

When he asked, Tom just shrugged. "I've been where you are," was all he would say. His pocket watch beeped, and Tom opened it. "I have to go."

Paul clasped the other man's hand and shook it, not even flinching at the electric tingling this time. "Thanks for everything."

Tom lifted his lantern. "If you ever need me, you know where I am." Then he lifted his hat and disappeared.

"Does that mean you're staying?" Ethan asked Paul hopefully.

"I'll be with you until we get to the hospital," replied the paramedic, not looking at Ethan as he checked the kid's IV.

Ethan held back laughter.

Paul grinned. "Yup. I'm here to stay."

"Cool," Ethan replied, relaxing into the stretcher. "It's nice to have someone around. You know, to help." Ethan looked unexpectedly fragile as he said this, and Paul realized that the kid had been on his own for a long time with no one but a chubby golden lab to look out for him.

Well, no more, Paul thought, settling onto the bench seat as the ambulance began to move, fully aware of the irony that he was only now turning his life around—the morning *after* his death.

KATRINA NICHOLSON is a freelance writer who also works for the Cape Breton Regional Library. Her screenplay *The Wild Helicopters of the Outback* took first place in the 5th Annual StoryPros Awards, and her novel *Unobtanium* won second place in the YA category of the 35th Atlantic Writing Competition. Her short film script *iBrain* was recently produced in Toronto. She has eight published short stories, which you

Katrina Nicholson

can find in Third Person Press's Speculative Elements series as well as in the anthologies *Tesseracts Fifteen*, *Futuredaze*, and *Future Embodied*. Check out her movie reviews site at www.refrigeratorbox.org.

Don't Miss
THE SPECULATIVE ELEMENTS SERIES
from
Third Person Press

Volume 1: *Undercurrents*

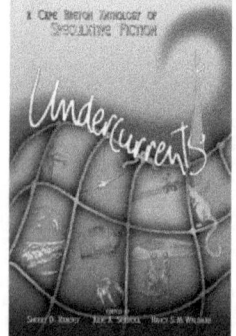

The landscape of Cape Breton writing doesn't necessarily begin at the Canso Causeway and end at the Cabot Strait. The fourteen stories in Undercurrents ply the literary oceans of time and space, possibility and imagination.

Inside are stories that ripple and swell with the unusual: fiddle-playing ghosts, malevolent cats, urbane vampires, and ordinary folks who have drifted into realms of the extraordinary.

"The 14 short stories cover every genre from laser blasting space opera to murder mystery ghost stories to Twilight Zone-esque creepers....Many of the writers found surprising ways to use the title of the collection as a theme in their tales." ~ Ken Chisholm, Cape Breton Post

Volume 2: *Airborne*

Stories and poems that breathe unexpected possibilities into the atmosphere that surrounds and fills us. Take flight with these tales and explore what is always elusive: microscopic particles, airwaves, wind, space, sound, and spirit.

These talented writers—all with a connection to Cape Breton Island—share stories of timeless love, enchanted flight, punkish cybercrime, unexpected gifts of healing, journeys beyond imagining, past lives on Scottish Isles, the knock at the door you never want to answer, and much more.

Don't Miss

THE SPECULATIVE ELEMENTS SERIES

from
Third Person Press

Volume 3: *Unearthed*

EARTH—the ground of our being, the dust from which we come and to which we will return. Imagine what might arise from and disappear into the soil...what grows, what is buried, what teems unseen.

This collection, exploring the ends of the Earth and beyond, offers tales from the depths of darkness: zombies, vampires, murky unknowable worlds, underground prisons, malevolent spirits—to the lightest heights: earthen magic, little people, buried treasure and fantastical creatures!

"After reading this book you will never look at things as normal as grass, mud, herbs, or even your own home the same way again. Prepare to have all of your hidden thoughts, worries, and questions unearthed." ~ Derek Newman-Stille, Speculating Canada

Coming in 2014:
Volume 4: *Flashpoint*

Books from **Third Person Press** available in print and ebook formats at
- thirdpersonpress.com
- amazon.ca/.com
- Smashwords
- and most other online outlets

Ask for our books in fine stores around Cape Breton Island.

Third
Person
Press

Also from Third Person Press:

To Unimagined Shores
Collected Stories by Sherry D. Ramsey

What sorts of things wash up on unimagined shores? Hitch-hiking aliens. Kidnapped embryos. Victorian time-machines. Spaceport detectives. Itinerant scribes. Otherworldly companions.

The discerning beachcomber will discover even more curiosities on the pages within: physicists and journalists, wizards and apprentices, angels and devils, telepaths and aliens. The seventeen stories in this collection are by turns funny, tragic, light-hearted and serious, but all share this in common: they will carry you to distant shores of imagination, and, once there, show you things you hadn't known before.

"Sherry D. Ramsey's short stories are filled with vibrant characters, good writing, and thrum with humanity, even when there aren't many actual humans in the story. Fans of speculative fiction should definitely check out To Unimagined Shores.*"~* Mark A. Rayner, author of *The Amadeus Net* and *Marvellous Hairy.*

Books from **Third Person Press**
available in print and ebook formats at
- thirdpersonpress.com
- amazon.ca/.com
- Smashwords
- and most other online outlets

Ask for our books in fine stores around Cape Breton Island.

www.ingramcontent.com/pod-product-compliance
Lightning Source LLC
Chambersburg PA
CBHW051834020726
47502CB00005B/1770